Electricity buzzes around us, and for a second, I swear there's no oxygen left in the car. He drops my hand and shifts in his seat. I'm staring at him, my new heart pounding in my chest. Something happens between us in that quiet instant, but I can't name it. It's almost…something.

PRAISE FOR THE WORKS OF SHARON M. JOHNSTON

"As Mishca's life unfolds, you pick up on a few eyebrow raises. *Divided* is an intriguing story that left me curious with what would be happening next."

- ECLIPSE REVIEWS

"*Divided* is a fast-paced adventure filled with mystery, romance, action, and humor. Mishca and Ryder rank up there with my favorite heroines and heroes ever! Sharon M. Johnston is an author to watch out for."

- *USA Today* & *New York Times* bestselling author, WENDY HIGGINS.

"*Divided* develops a unique and intriguing storyline and will keep you guessing the possible outcome."

- Author and Artist, NIKOLA VUKOJA

"Wow. Just wow. *Divided* is such a great story. It's a slow burn. You think you've got it all figured out and then there's a right hook followed by a quick left and jab to the ribs."

- YA Author, CRYSTAL COLLIER

SHARON M. JOHNSTON

DIVIDED

AN OPEN HEART NOVEL

Book One

CITY OWL
PRESS

DIVIDED
An Open Heart Novel: Book One

CITY OWL PRESS
www.cityowlpress.com

For information on subsidiary rights, please contact the publisher at info@cityowlpress.com.

Print Edition ISBN: 978-0-9862516-3-4

Printed in the United States of America

For She-Who-Must-Not-be-Named.

Without you there would be no book.

- Sharon

CHAPTER 1

SOMEONE MUST DIE so I can live. I've come to terms with that. Before it turned my stomach, thinking about my donor's death, but now I'm used to it. Most likely, it'll be a car accident or a drunken fall. It won't come from illness or any other natural causes that corrupt human organs and make the deceased ineligible to be a donor. A violent, painful death will be my savior. It's the only way I'll ever get my new heart.

I open my eyes and stare upward, hoping the white fluffy clouds splotched against the blue sky will distract me from my imaginings of people dying. I guess I'm not as used to the idea of getting someone else's heart as I thought. The harsh Australian sun makes me squint.

I swing my legs around and hoist myself upright on the stadium bleacher, looking over the sports field. Readjusting my tank top strap that had slipped off my shoulder, I try to conjure up happier thoughts. At least I won't be responsible for the person who dies, even if I get a new heart out of the mess.

Yeah, happier thoughts.

A sigh escapes. This isn't how I expected to be spending my first year out of high school, watching my dad as he puts hopeful rugby league players through their paces. It's been that and hanging out with Mum at home. My friends have taken a gap year, backpacking through Europe. The seasons are the exact opposite in the Northern Hemisphere to Australia, so spring in October here is autumn in Europe. All my friends are watching leaves turn orange and spiral to the ground, while I sweat it out at home. When Mum and Dad found out I was near the top of the transplant list, they insisted I still take a year off, but vetoed my plans to join my friends in case someone croaked. *A lovely thought.* So all my friends left, minus me. I've barely heard from them during the past eight months. And most of them won't be back for at least another few weeks, just before Christmas.

I don't hold it against Mum and Dad. *Even though, a rugby arena isn't my idea of a good time. But whatever.* They do it because they care. They've proved time and time again you don't need blood ties to be great parents or overprotective ones. Mum jokes that if we get the call soon about a heart for me it'll be an early Christmas present. *Will someone die in the next month? I really don't want to be in the hospital over Christmas.* I purse my lips and twitch my mouth side-to-side, trying to push away the insidious thought.

"All right, boys. That wraps it up for today," Dad calls out to the pack of sweaty guys. "Hit the showers, and I'll see you all tomorrow."

I do my best not to ogle as the group heads in my direction. Half of them are shirtless, their muscles glistening after the training session. Okay, so I'm totally staring. A cute red-haired guy catches me gawking and winks. I simper at him in a lame attempt at sexy. A guy I went to school with nudges Cutie Ginger and shakes his head. I suppress a huff. I believed with the end of an era, I could have a fresh start, but it appears my reputation will haunt me beyond high school. *Mishca the Untouchable.*

Dad lingers behind, deep in discussions with the managers and trainers; no doubt talking over the fates of the young men desperate to break into the rugby league at a national level. They were all trying so hard to get Coach Tom Richardson's attention. If only I had that many guys chasing after me. If only I had *any* guys chasing after me.

I pat the edges of my almost-afro to make sure it doesn't look like I've stuck my finger in an electric socket.

Finally, Dad makes his way to me, leaving his

entourage behind.

"Any contenders in your latest batch of victims?" I ask, picking up my discarded copy of *West Side Story*. I'd been rereading my university audition piece, torturing myself on how I could have performed it better. There was no way I was putting off uni for another year, new heart or no new heart. I wish I had tried out for plays at school, but I remained a closet actor, only performing in drama class for fear somehow my weak disposition would get in the way. Next year, I swear, will be different. A new heart and new hope—surely someone suitable will die soon. I wince at how heartless that sounds.

"There may be some," Dad replies, humoring me and fully aware I have little interest in his latest player acquisitions. He puts his hand on my shoulder. "I've got to grab some paperwork from the office before we go."

"Sure thing," I say to his back as he retreats up the stadium tunnel. I trudge behind him, my book clutched in my hand.

With each step the tips of my curls brush lightly against my bare shoulders. It tickles and I regret agreeing with Mum to grow it out. Appeasing her is my attempt to bridge the gap between us. Or so I rationalize. But it's like the more I align my thinking with Mum's the more I can show the world I am truly her daughter, despite how different we look and sharing no DNA. I shove my hands into the pockets of my denim shorts and focus on the blissful shade I'll get once I'm inside.

My nose wrinkles when I step through the door. The whole place smells like dude, and not in a good sense, but in the human male equivalent of a stinky wet dog. I hold my nose, walk down the corridor, and lean against the cool cement wall outside Dad's office. I sneak a peek down the hall. *Naked guys. There are naked guys right down there. The closest I've been to male nudity of a datable age.* I bite my lower lip. Stupid heart ruins my life, as usual.

My heart transplant operation is like a ticking time bomb waiting to go off, but without a countdown to watch. I can't help but wonder. Would my parents still have wanted to adopt me if they'd known I had a congenial heart disease — this hole in my heart? Do they regret adopting me with all that baggage?

A voice floats down from the locker room, invading my thoughts. "That girl was hot. Who was she? I could love on some brown sugar."

I squee inside, hoping it's the Ron Weasley look-a-like.

"Seriously, don't go there. Apart from being Coach Richardson's daughter, she's got a broken heart, and I mean literally. Mishca couldn't even play sports at school cause it might've killed her. There's no way you can hit that. She might die on you during sex, and you'd be left screwing a corpse."

"You're kidding me?" His eyebrows rise. "Thanks, man. Dodged a bullet there."

I suck in a breath and run down the corridor to the seating. A mini cyclone of rage mixes inside me with a swirl of sadness, both fighting for control. Part of me fights not to breakdown and cry while the other half holds back a scream and the insistent urge to pummel any guy that comes near. Instead, I throw my playbook onto a chair, curl my fists, and stand rigid. My breath comes in ragged gulps and my chest burns. *Stupid weak heart! It's gotten in the way for so long. I wish someone would die...right... now.*

My fist connects with the wall in a feeble push. *Crap, that hurts!* I blow on my now pink knuckles to ease the throbbing. *Note to self, UFC isn't the career for you.* I flick my hand about as though it will disperse the pain.

"Mishca!"

Dad races toward me. Something's up...or he's extremely happy. His face morphs between the two emotions faster than I can tell. He stops in front of me and grabs my hands. I glance down trying not to wince at the pain from my pink knuckles and hoping he doesn't notice.

"What's going on, Dad?"

He looks me in the eye and rubs his thumb over my hand. "They've got a donor. It's time."

CHAPTER 2

"HOW NICE THAT YOU'RE coming to give your friend support," says the nurse to my mother, handing the hospital admission forms to me.

"She's my daughter," snaps Mum as she snatches up the clipboard and starts poring over it. I shift my weight as though it will allow my discomfort from the misunderstanding and my mum's reaction to slide off me.

Dad gives the nurse an apologetic nod. It's an easy mistake to make, and one made all too often. Not many people would pick me as the daughter of a blond Australian supermodel. I look more like I should be Lenny Kravitz's kid.

I glance sideways at her. She's not taking this whole your-daughter-needs-a-heart-transplant saga well. *Come on, Mum. Get it together for once, for me.* The pen shakes between my mum's delicate fingers, threatening to rattle against her gold rings. She attempts to fill in the paperwork.

"You don't have to do that, Mum," I attempt to keep my voice even. "I'm nineteen now, I have to sign this myself anyway."

"No," she replies. "You've got enough to deal with."

I wonder how long she'll be able to keep this up. Mum and stress are not friends. Inevitably, she falls into a drama-filled pile of goo that Dad has to nurture back into the form of a functional person. It's exhausting for all of us.

She continues staring at the paperwork without writing anymore. If anyone doubted my mother's strong denial of plastic surgery, they'd only need to check her out now to see the truth. Her forehead creases as she studies the form.

Is there any family history of heart disease, diabetes, high cholesterol, or high blood pressure?

I watch with intent to see what she'll do. The only sections she fills in with confidence are my personal details, immunization history, and that I don't smoke and I'm not pregnant.

Mum pushes the board holding the uncompleted form to the nurse with a faint, "I'm sorry," and rushes out of the hospital reception room, dragging me behind. I roll my eyes at Dad. He gives me a rueful shrug, mouths that he'll catch up, and then turns to the nurse. I huff and let Mum yank me further away from the desk. *Not today, Mum. Please. This is hard enough.* I squish my eyes tight, willing the ungrateful thoughts away. If someone without my parents' level of wealth had adopted me, I might already be dead. They've given so much to help with my medical condition.

We move so quickly down the blinding white hallways that my chest tightens and my breath turns raspy. Shooting pains attack my ribs. I want to slow down, but reminding Mum about my defective heart won't help the situation. Her falling in a heap on the floor and making an even bigger scene would compound things.

We escape from the claustrophobic corridors into the front garden, snagging a park bench nestled in the nearby foliage. People going by would pick my mother as the one nearing death's door rather than me. I hug Mum to me, breathing sharply as my chest continues to sear in protest. More than her slight frame pushes against me. The guilt of my defective heart, the anger at Mum's ability to play the victim, the fear of going under the knife, all of it suffocates me. I gasp for air, resisting the urge to shove Mum off me and onto the ground so I can scream at her.

Deep breaths. 1...2...3...4...5... I inhale and exhale, willing my heart to slow. *You know that's how she is.* When I can get it into a semi-steady rhythm, I gasp, "Mum?"

She angles her tear-stained face toward me with

that startled kangaroo-in-headlights expression. The shame of her breakdown starts to creep along her cheeks in shades of pink. She reaches out and pulls a flower from the surrounding hedges, methodically plucking off the petals.

I want to grab her head and make her look me in the eye. I need her now, more than I've even needed her before. *Come on. Look at me, Mum.* I wait a heartbeat. When she doesn't comply with my unspoken demand, I sigh and try to catch her attention with a question.

"Mum, won't the adoption records have my health history in them?"

She freezes as though she's searching for the right words. Before she can respond, Dad strides over from the hospital entrance and grabs us both in a massive bear hug. I sag into him; my head against his chest, letting him absorb all my anger, all my fear. Tears trickle down my cheeks, but I won't let them overtake me. I need to be strong so I can face what's waiting for me in the operating room. The rapid thumping of my heart eases until it beats in a steady duet with Dad's. Mum's hair falls like a veil protecting me from the world.

After a collective deep breath, we separate, Mum easing her head from Dad's shoulder before I extract myself as well. Surveying them both, I straighten my spine. I'm determined to get answers this time.

"Won't my medical history be in the adoption papers?" I repeat my earlier question.

Dad shakes his head, and Mum's hand flies to her mouth as though to suppress a sob.

"It wasn't a regular adoption, Mishca. At the time, we chose a more," Dad pauses searching the sky for the words, "selective agency. We'd heard of other cases where the birth parents became too involved after recognizing their child with a celebrity parent. The service had additional security, but it went both ways. We were given the bare minimum of information about you, and the birth parents knew nothing about us. We knew you were from a mixed race couple in the United States who couldn't keep you." Dad's eyes glisten and his words catch in his throat. "We wanted you so badly. At that time it worked well for everyone."

The words sink in deep. My starved mind eats up each one like an inedible morsel of food. I stare at the ground. My gaze flickers to Mum's stomach as it always does when I think of the baby they lost before they adopted me.

"This isn't the first time I've been admitted into the hospital and we haven't had all the information. It's not like Dr. Thompson won't operate on me because he doesn't know if diabetes runs in my family, right?" I try my best to sound reassuring, even though part of me wants to run away as fast as I can and hide. But I can't run more than 100 meters without wheezing, and I suck at hide-and-seek.

Mum's face relaxes. "We have the best doctor, the best hospital in Brisbane, and it isn't like this operation hasn't been performed successfully before." She manages the first smile I've seen from her today and it's enough for us to head inside. Dad tackles the form with advice from the nurse. I work on keeping Mum calm, still wishing it were the other way around.

It takes less time than I expect before I'm in the unflattering hospital gown and hugging Mum and Dad goodbye. Then, a nurse bustles me onto the gurney. I want to watch my parents until the last second, but seeing their tears will break me apart. I can't run from things like Mum. I have to take this chance to live a normal life. I focus on the florescent lights in the ceiling until the orderlies wheel me to my final destination.

When we enter the stark stainless steel lined operating room I long for the comfort of the warm waiting room. I expect to wake up a bit sore and sorry after the operation, but how much pain will there be? I have no idea and it makes my insides tighten. A niggling thought tells me to make peace with my maker because it could be my last chance. So I do. But that small thought gets much bigger — and a helluva a lot scarier — in the reality of the operating room.

The medical team mills around. No one says a

word to me until it's time to go under, leaving me feeling like a piece of meat. I gulp as the doctor asks me to count back from ten. I make it to nine.

Voices drift around me. Murmurs and faint whispers flow through my mind, but I lack the focus to hold on to them. A blanket of fog embraces me, pulling me into what I thought would be nothingness.

I run into blackness. An intense guilt weighs me down. Guilty… wrong… bad… the words ripple around me, filling my soul with emotions. What had I done? What did I do to warrant this shame? I want to turn to the light. Don't take me away from the light.

My eyelids flutter open still thick with drug-induced sleep. I see my mother leaning against the wall, twirling the ends of her hair between her fingers. Dad sits in a chair off to the side.

I attempt to rise from the pillow to greet her, but the pain makes me weak and I sink back to the bed.

"She's awake." I roll my eyes. *Way to state the obvious, Mum.*

Dad rushes to my side and kisses my forehead. I shake my head, not wanting to return to the freaky drug-induced dream. I shiver at the memory. When you are close to dying, don't you run to the light?

I need to breathe. I need air.

The corners of my mouth turn to smile, but I end up wincing instead as I fumble to find the bed controls. I force my body into a sitting position while pain shoots through my chest. My new medical silverware jingles on my wrist when I reach out to clasp Dad's outstretched hand. Hmmm, not very fashionable, but I'm not surprised Mum made sure I was sporting it before regaining consciousness.

"How are you feeling?" Dad asks.

"Good," I croak out, but my eyelids want to droop and the painkillers take control again, drawing me back into darkness.

A beam of moonlight streams through the window, leaving a silver streak in the middle of my otherwise dim hospital room. Gingerly, I sit up and recoil with horror at the multiple tubes protruding from my mouth, nose, and arms. My arms flail at them to detach. A burning sensation rips through my throat in protest as blood drips from my wrist. The night calls to me and I make my way to the open window. A cool breeze drifts past.

A sound behind makes me jump. I turn to see shadows flitting past the door. Malevolent gales of laughter echo down the corridor. I press myself against the wall next to the window as a sinister outline peeks around the corner.

"You'll never be good enough, Mishca." Clammy hands reach through the panes and grip my throat.

"Never. Good. Enough," the voice whispers into my ear.

I wake, punching at the empty space above me. *Breathe, calm down.* I suck the air in long ragged gasps, and gradually, my heartbeat steadies. Even in the gloomy hospital room I can make out the silhouette of Dad in the corner, sleeping in the visitor chair. His soft snores fill the void and wrap around me like a safety blanket. Yet my skin prickles a warning.

Something bad is coming.

CHAPTER 3

DR. THOMPSON TOLD ME I would notice a difference with my new heart, but I didn't expect it to be *this* immediate. I have more energy than I've ever had and am itching to get out of the hospital. Improved health isn't the only thing that's changed. Facing my mortality has fueled my desire to find out about my birth parents. I've never cared who my DNA donators were before, but I could've inherited my weak old heart from their genes. I know nothing about them, which means there's a lot about me I don't know.

I want to know everything. I want to do everything! Yet despite how healthy I feel, something is off. Uneasiness sits at the back of my mind. I can't work out why, or what it is, but it's there. I remain on high alert, analyzing my actions, trying to decipher if my sixth sense has any truth to it, or if the operation has sent me to paranoid city.

I've only been in here for a couple of days, and I want to be anywhere else. At least now I'm out of the intensive care unit and in my own room for the next two weeks. The pastel aqua walls adorned with paintings of soothing nautical scenes are a welcome change. Unfortunately, the bright cheery room has done nothing to stave off the nightmares I've had since my operation—or help my boredom. Spending all day in bed isn't as much fun as I thought it would be, even with the big pile of books Mum has supplied. She did get me a good mix of classic novels and plays.

I avoid scratching my itchy chest, but I can't help peeking down my hospital robe. I drop the fabric and… the sight; it's too much. I avert my gaze to the window. Concrete arches and ledges fill the view, but they don't seem to match the exterior walls I remember. When we entered the hospital, the bricks I saw were small and orange. Yet as I crane my neck now for a better view, I see a combination of stone and concrete that makes up intricate patterns like those on old European buildings.

On the ledge sit a number of gargoyles, ranging in size and features from small and grotesque to large and less monstrous. One in particular catches my eye. More man than beast and, except for the wings, tail, and horns, it could pass for an ancient warrior. With my curiosity piqued, I seize the opportunity when the nurse comes in with my next lot of pills.

"Excuse me? Can you tell me what that is out there?" I motion to the array of statues outside my window. "It's so different from the rest of the hospital."

The nurse beams at me. "What you can see out there, sweetheart, is the prayer room and chaplaincy area. It's where family and friends go when they need some comfort. Patients can go there too." She pauses to read my chart, and then adds, "When they're well enough."

I raise an eyebrow at her. I feel healthier than I've ever been in my life. I think I could make it to the chapel.

"Here, you need to take your next round of meds now," she continues in her peppy voice.

I stare at the door, fear clawing up my stomach into my throat. Mum and Dad haven't returned from the cafeteria yet, and I don't want to be dead to the world when they get back.

"Will these make me sleepy?" I ask, doing my best to keep my voice level.

"Yes, dear," she says reassuringly, even though it's not what I want to hear. "Rest is an important part of the recovery process."

I bite my lip, trying to work out a way to stall. Fortunately, two familiar faces peep around the corner. Dad sits on the bed beside me and pats my hand as the pills kick in. I hope having him so close will ward off the nightmares.

It doesn't.

"You killed her, Mishca," whispers a voice through the fog that surrounds me. "She needed to die so you could live."

I whip around to try and get a glimpse of Mr. Creepy Voice, the regular narrator of my nightmares. Mist greets me.

"Who are you? What do you want with me?" I call out.

My own voice echoes. I take a step forward and my foot connects with something. A limp form lies in the dirt. Flowing blond hair frames a beautiful and peaceful face. I let my gaze slide from the closed eyes, to roam across her cheeks, and down over her nakedness. I want to turn away but am rooted to the spot, staring at the red stains zigzagging her porcelain skin and the bloody hole in her chest — right where her heart should be.

Her eyes flash open.

"You killed me."

Groaning, I wipe the moist layer of sweat from my forehead. I don't like being awake in the middle of the night in a strange bed, especially after a dream like that. The IV drip annoys me more than my stitches. I yearn to rip it from my hand but stare at the ceiling instead.

Disturbed by the prospect of returning to the dream, I decide to stretch my legs. I grab my IV stand and exit, wheeling out and shivering as the cool air-conditioning lowers my body temperature. My thoughts drift to the chapel, craving the inner peace that'll let me shake off the nightmares. I inch toward the sanctuary.

Wooziness ripples over me. I grab at the door handle and stumble. A cracking noise coincides with a lump of hard metal falling into my hands. My eyes widen at the door handle. *Did I do that? No way. The door must be faulty.* For how much my parents are paying for this hospital, you'd think they could maintain the place in decent condition. I drop it on the floor. The cleaners will find it during their rounds.

I shuffle down the corridor and through the double doors that lead to Dr. Thompson's offices. I'm sure we passed a sign pointing to the chapel when we went to my appointments.

"You should not be here."

Huh? I turn around, trying to pinpoint the voice's location.

Nothing. I'm alone.

"It's not for you to say where I can be," says another voice.

I glance around again, but there's no one. My skin prickles when I spot the chapel entrance. I stop short. Heated voices come from within.

How did I hear their voices all the way down the hallway? I shake my head. It can't be the same people. I was probably imagining things with my meds.

An odd tingling overtakes my toes, traveling up my body. I shake my arms and wiggle my legs to make the sensation go away. But it doesn't. Not wanting to interrupt, but too curious to leave, I linger near the door. The people inside don't sound happy.

"I am observing, not interfering."

"She is evidence of your interference. Leave this place at once," the first voice says in a tone that makes it clear it's not a request but a demand.

"Honestly, I don't see what all of the fuss is about," chimes in a female voice. She sounds so familiar, but I can't place her. "She's a defective human."

"Othilia, you were once like her," the first voice says. "You made your choice, and she must make hers."

I move closer, contemplating a sneak peek into the room.

"Wait," says the female voice. "I feel her."

I freeze, not wanting to be seen. *Whoa. What a bunch of weirdos.* My heart stops. *What the – ?* There's no one else in sight, but they can't be talking about me. My attempt at self-assurance doesn't stop me from backing away. *Don't be stupid, how can you "feel" someone anyway?* Their conversation makes no sense. Probably someone else in the chapel I didn't hear. I start walking, about to retreat to my room, when a hand touches my shoulder.

"Are you okay?" A short young guy gives me a smile. He pushes shaggy brown hair from across his green eyes.

"Yeah, I'm fine." I gesture to the chapel. "I was going to go inside, but it's a busy night apparently."

"Really? I'm sure there's always room for one more in the house of the Lord." He says it so loud I want to shush him.

"Oh no, it's okay. They sound, um, busy."

"God's house has many rooms," he says in a tone that would draw dirty glares from a librarian. "Let's go in and talk."

A clerical collar and cross hang around his neck. He doesn't appear old enough to be a priest or a pastor, despite his getup. No sound comes from the chapel now, but I don't move. No one has come out.

"Um, maybe some other time."

"Are you sure? You look like you could use a cup of hot chocolate with marshmallows." He peers around the doorway. "The room's empty now."

Is he sure? Where did they go? I wonder but don't ask. "As awesome as that sounds, I'd better get going before the nurses send a search party."

"Okay. Well, if you change your mind, I'm on duty here for the next two weeks. Ask for Markus." He holds out his hand. I slip mine into his and give a limp shake. His skin heats like an inferno.

"Sure thing," I reply, not meaning the words.

He waves goodbye as I withdraw to my room, all the while thinking over the strangers' odd conversation about an unknown *she*.

CHAPTER 4

IT'S BEEN FOUR WEEKS since my operation and the bad dreams have been with me every night since I...well, I technically died on the operating table. Every time I think about it my stomach threatens to expel its contents. I want to wipe it from my mind, but the nightmares don't let me forget.

At the end of the bed Smelly Belly eyes me in the arched position, her hair standing on end. I hope that cat stare is from my thrashing about in my sleep and not from screaming.

I register something nasty in my hand—the liquid from my lava lamp that normally sits on my bedside table. I've squeezed it so hard the glass broke and the gooey insides have spilled over me and the pile of books beside my bed. Luckily, it wasn't on so the globs haven't burned me, and I've somehow avoided cutting my hand on the glass shards.

WTF! How did I do that? Gross. I grab tissues and swipe at it.

Footsteps thud down the hall. I scramble to push a sheet over the goo and glass. My dad bolts into the room.

Nope. I sigh. *Definitely must have been screaming.*

"Mishca? Is everything okay?" He surveys the room and goes off red alert mode when he sees no immediate danger. The sheet cover must be working, but if he stays too long I'm afraid the waxy smell will set him on alert again.

"I'm fine. A bit of a nightmare, that's all." I suck on my bottom lip and avoid eye-contact. I haven't told my parents about the dreams plaguing me since my heart transplant. *No need to worry them. They're dreams after all. Right?*

As though he didn't hear me, Dad strides over and sits on the bed. He rests his hand on a sweaty patch and screws up his face in a silent *eww*. At least he's not sitting on the remains of the lava lamp. "You remember Dr. Thompson said we need to tell him if anything unusual happens. He wants to monitor the side effects of your medication."

"Uh-huh." I shrug and focus on the wall instead of Dad's face.

"So you were having lots of bad dreams before the operation?" He sounds concerned, but why ask? He knows I wasn't.

"No," I whisper. "I'll tell him next visit."

At least Dad hasn't noticed the bizarre accidents. It's like I'm jinxed. I keep breaking things just by touching them. It's driving me insane.

Dad clears his throat and places his hand on mine. I try not to fixate on the difference in our coloring. Sometimes I can forget for a while, but too often it reminds me…I'm not like my parents. He pats my hand. "How 'bout you put those sheets in the laundry for May-Lee? No need to worry your mother. I'll get you a fresh set."

He heads out the door to the linen cupboard. Like I need some messed up dream to bring me down today. My plans for tonight already feel like a betrayal.

I check the time. Nearly six in the morning. No point in going back to sleep when my alarm will be going off in an hour anyway. I make quick work of disposing the lava lamp remains and hiding the rest before Dad returns with a set of blue sheets. I'll have to vacuum up the other bits after he leaves. For now I keep the dirty sheet covering what's left of the mess.

Handing the clean sheets to me, Dad grins. "You mightn't think your old man is cool anymore, but you can talk to me if something's bothering you. Problems aren't meant to be dealt with alone." He reaches out, tussles my messy hair, and retreats. His words clang around in my head like a hollow bell. I know they love me. Everything should be perfect now, and I don't want to ruin things with weirdness. When I say nothing, he adds, "Okay then. Hope you have sweeter dreams tonight."

The sweat still sticks my clothes to my skin. The tiles cool my feet as I head to the bathroom for a lukewarm shower. Hot ones are off limits. Doc said they might raise my blood pressure too much while I'm recovering from the surgery.

I let the water wash away the clamminess and the bad dream. My new heart has given me new life. I wouldn't change that, but the medication side effects are starting to irk me.

"Stupid dreams." I mutter under the shower's spray. "Stupid accidents." I guess they're better than what I went through before the operation, being so sick and weak. And the panic attacks. The most awful shitty panic attacks ever. At least that's what the doctor thought they were.

They started one day out of nowhere. A sudden sadness would consume me, swallowing me whole. Then, I'd scream in pain because it felt like I was being ripped apart inside, like a piece of me was being hacked off. Mum and Dad recorded more than twenty of them from the time I was about ten-years-old. There was no pattern, just sporadic episodes. When they ran the tests for the attacks, they found my heart condition.

Good news? No more of those episodes. Haven't

had a one since my transplant. Small favors, I guess.

I turn off the taps very carefully to make sure they don't break in my hands like so many other things I've destroyed lately, and try to focus on anything but my medical problems. It's hard to do with an angry red scar running down my chest like a crimson railroad track. I dry over it quickly so I can cover it with clothes. First up, a change into my workout outfit of leggings and a fitted purple t-shirt. Mum's been watching me like a hawk to make sure I stick to the fitness regimen Dr. Thomas assigned.

I go to my room to get my shoes and stop at the sight of my laptop. My finger flicks over the touch screen and it springs to life. I go straight to the same web page I've been obsessing about since my operation—the adoption agency website, Eleithyia Elite Family Services. I scan the ad of an available adoptee: *"Beautiful baby girl of African-American origin, due for adoption mid-January."* That could've been me nineteen years ago. The description fits with my features: brown skin, smoky almond eyes, and a mass of curls. Why did her parents give her up? Why did my parents give me up? The desire to find my birthparents burns so bright since my operation.

"Tonight," I whisper. "It starts tonight."

I force my pointer away from the page, opening Facebook instead in the hope it will distract me. My user name is Ms. Chief—a compromise with my parents to "keep me safe" after a recent extortion attempt against one of their friends that involved threats to their son. The daughter of a model and rugby league coach could be the next mark in my mother's opinion. She's being overly dramatic, but I humor her. Nothing exciting in the notifications, but there's a weird message in my inbox from a Belinda Fielding. I slip my shoes on and start lacing them up as I read.

Hi, I was wondering if you're Michelle Cooper who went to Mackay North State High School? I'm trying to track her down. You look just like her and Mischief was her nickname at school. Cheers, Belinda.

Sorry, I type in response, *Mishca from Brisbane.*

It's not the first time I've been mistaken for someone else, but it's usually guys who follow up with a friend request. Creepy.

I log off, still thinking about the message. I'm not sure if my doppelganger exists because I've never seen anyone so similar they could be mistaken for me. Although, when I did a full afro for an underage rave, I enjoyed the Beyoncé in *Austin Powers* style comments.

The smell of frying bacon wafts into my room, taking away the remnant aroma of the lava lamp incident. *Boy, I miss bacon. Stupid low-sodium, low-fat diet.* My mouth waters. Dad can be a sadist at times, but I understand. He didn't have the heart transplant, so why should he miss out on his favorite foods? He'd slept in the downstairs guest room for two nights after the fight with Mum about it until I convinced her to let him upstairs again.

I put on my shoes, and then grab my iPhone, headphones, and exercise armband so I can start my workout straight after breakfast. But my feet stop at the top of the stairs, and I wonder if it would be better to hole up in my room a bit longer. I'm not sure if I can handle Mum this morning, especially after that dream. She's always on my case about exercise, vitamins, and medicine, or hassling Dad since the operation. I'm still walking on eggshells after our argument a couple of days ago. She's worried there'll be too many germs at university next year and that I should defer. Honestly, my life's been on hold long enough. She should be happy I'm going to school in Brisbane and not out of state so she can still have me at home. If I thought my parents would pay for me to live on campus, I'd ask. It's not like money is an issue, but Mum's made it crystal she wants me super close until I get the complete all-clear from Dr. Thompson.

I walk through the lounge room, staring at the wilting flowers waiting to be replaced. Normally, this is the happiest room in our Highgate Hill house with walls of white that glisten from the reflection of the sun off the pool, and the calming sound of water lapping against the stone wall at the base of our riverfront home. Today, it's somber. Overcast skies hide the sunshine and dull the room.

As I enter the kitchen, Smelly Belly pads in a slinky, snake-like way between my legs, no doubt hoping for some bacon.

"Decided to join us, huh?" Dad grins at me as he turns a slice of sizzling bacon. The toaster pops to his right. "You want some toast?"

I shake my head. "Nah, I'll have fruit." In the fridge is a bowl of cut fruit Mum must've prepared earlier, even though she's nowhere in sight. I pull out a stool from under the bench.

"Got big plans for the summer?" Dad asks between munches of bacon.

I shrug. My recovery time will allow me to enjoy the months I have off before university starts.

"Not too much, hanging out with friends and stuff." *If they still even remember who I am.* I try to sound chipper.

"That sounds like fun." Dad grins. "Did you see this?"

He shoves the paper under my nose and points to an article about a local theater group holding auditions for *The Sound of Music*. Nice, seeing as he normally pooh-poohs my interest in drama, though he obviously hasn't thought it through.

"Ah, I'm the wrong color for that one, Dad."

He peers at me, but before he can say anything the harsh trill of our home phone rings throughout the house. Mum appears, scurrying to answer it.

She picks up, walks into the next room, and starts talking to one of her fashion pals. I focus hard and pick up the conversation. *Wow, new heart and improved hearing. Double bonus.* Doubt wiggles at the back of my mind, a lingering unease.

Why would the operation result in me having crazy-ass hearing? I tug at my hair, warring with myself. *Oh, shut-up and try to be normal for once.*

"No, you can't come over, not until your cold has cleared." Mum pauses in her phone conversation. "I'm serious, she's still too fragile."

Hello, right here! I stare daggers at the wall between us but say nothing.

"Okay, I'll meet you for lunch there. See you then."

Soft sobbing follows. I can't help but let out a groan before shoving some more food in my mouth. She's the one who should be into drama with all her theatrics. As much as I love my mother, she's managed to make this about her. Since the operation she's shed more tears than me. The emotional exhaustion from pulling her out of a funk all the time has left me flat like a deflated balloon.

"Mishca, honey?" Mum comes into the kitchen, sniffles, and dabs at her green eyes. "I'm not feeling too well. I'm going to lay down for a bit. Would you be able to call Dr. Thompson to confirm your next checkup? I'm not up to it."

I don't say anything. I don't have to. My face

must say it all because Mum stops suppressing the tears and flees, her long blond hair flicking behind her.

I get up, scratching the stool across the tiled floor, and leave everything where it is for our housekeeper to clear away. It's not my standard MO, but I need to retreat to my room. Turning into a hermit isn't the best approach; of course, I can't deal with my parents right now. It's hard enough handling my own emotions without Dad giving me the old "give your mother some time" talk.

I stare at the bookmark in *Sense and Sensibility* but decide to do some eBay surfing, seeing as Mum isn't keen for me to go to the "germ-ridden" shops yet.

I flip open the laptop I'd discarded on the bed before breakfast, intent on purging my anger with purchases. But as soon as I open up the Internet I'm back on the Eleithyia Elite Family Services home page again. I stare at the descriptions of babies that will be up for adoption soon.

Why didn't you want me? My sadness swirls around me, pulling me down like quicksand. *So many. So many unwanted babies.*

A knock on my door makes me jump and disturbs Smelly Belly, who had been purring contentedly on my bed. I slam my laptop shut and fake fooling around on my phone as Dad pokes his head in the doorway.

"Hey, mind if I come in?"

I shrug and put on my armband for my phone in case I need to use my workout as a quick escape from the conversation. He sits on the bed and begins stroking the fur ball, who purrs in appreciation.

"How are you doing with everything?"

I don't respond, focusing on the content cat curled up on my bed.

"You look like you're all set for this morning's workout. Do you want some company?"

This time I shake my head.

"I know this is hard on you, but it isn't easy on your mother and me either." He has obviously been comforting *her* again.

I cock my eyebrow in response and slip my phone into the exercise band, doing my best impression of a cold-hearted bitch. If my stone façade cracks, what comes out could scare us both.

"Mishca, please, you need to cut her a bit of slack. She loves you very much. This has been difficult for her too."

"Don't even go there." I give him the speak-to-the-hand gesture, my rage rising. I struggle to keep control. I'm not normally quick to anger. Then again, my meds did say there could be mood swings.

No! I dismiss the meds, holding onto the root of the problem. *She's not being fair! This is not about her.*

It's about me!

Dad's features soften. "Do you need a rest? You haven't been sleeping well. I hear you up at all hours of the night."

I don't respond, folding my arms instead. Nightmares have nothing to do with this.

"Damn it, Mishca, she's trying. She's so scared of losing you. With everything that has happened, could you please—"

"It hasn't happened to her. It happened to me!" I jab my finger in the air at his face. "*I* was the one they sliced open. *I* was the one who technically died. And *I* am the one who has to wait to see if my body rejects my new heart or if it takes. So excuse me if I don't give a flying fuck about how *she* feels right now."

Something clicks inside me, a pull at my chest, an urgency to leave before a deeper anger bubbles over. I run.

Hot shame rises in waves through me, the tears streaking down my face provides no relief. I zigzag around the house to escape not only the confrontation but also the urge to smash things. Dad calls my name as he follows close behind. I expect his hands to grab me at any moment, but they never come. Dad pants behind me. The sound of his footsteps grows softer as I out pace him, creating a gap between us. It makes no sense he hasn't caught me. He's fast. Somehow, I'm faster.

May-Lee arrives as I reach the front yard, so the electronic gate at the driveway opens. Seizing the opportunity, I dart onto the footpath. My legs have a mind of their own. In fact, I never used to run much at all because it always resulted in chest pains. This time, though, my heart beats strongly, my lungs fill with air and I hit my stride. As I round the corner onto the main street I hear Dad yelling, but I don't even turn around.

CHAPTER 5

DON'T DRIVE MAD. It's good advice. But running mad is amazing. The time alone helps me compose my emotions after my fight with Dad. I love the wind brushing past my cheeks. I have no idea how fast I'm going, but it's like I've always run—natural, right, and so easy. Cruise control kicks in and I could go faster if I push it.

Thank you, new heart.

People glance, some stare, as I race past them at a speed that would put an Olympic sprinter to shame. The thought makes something settle low in my gut. I slow down, letting the situation sink in.

Are you an idiot? My mind races, realizing what I've done, and shouldn't be able to do. *No way. How could I run like that?*

Dr. Thompson did say I would feel different straight away. Part of me knows I'm kidding myself—the new heart wouldn't make that much of a difference, but I push the thought away. I've got too much to deal with as it is.

When my legs decide they've had enough, I find I'm in front of the Fitness Factory, a local sports store. An eerie tingling gives me goose bumps all over my skin and a sense of déjà vu. I contemplate going inside, but as I stare at the large glass entrance doors, something feels wrong.

The girl in the reflection isn't me.

At least, not quite me. My face stares back at me, almost impassively, but the *me* in the glass is all in black, looking leaner, harder, and stronger. My jaw drops. The *me* in the reflection smirks and wiggles her fingers before turning her hand and flipping me the bird.

I swing around to see if anyone else observes my creepy twin in the glass. No one seems to notice anything. The people coming through the door set off the sensor and walk straight in.

When the door closes again, the regular me stares back with a dumbfound expression.

W-T-F! My heart thuds against my ribcage as though to break through the bone and escape. *No! No more weird. No more different. It's my time to be normal.*

I dash inside to escape my reflection. With people all around me the sense of threat dissipates. I stand still, breathing deeply and ignoring the missed call coming from my cell. After a couple of minutes, I rationalize hallucinations are a listed side effect of my transplant drugs.

Great, I'm going to have to tell Dr. Thompson I've been hallucinating too.

Calmer, and hopefully saner, I decide I might as well do some window shopping. *September's not too early to buy Christmas presents, is it?* Not for Mum; she's probably got everyone's presents already. Plus, it gives me some more alone time. Thinking about Dad raises the guilt rise from my gut. *Maybe that's what you deserve.*

I glance at the aisle lists. A bit cliché for a rugby league coach, but I'm contemplating getting him something in opposition colors as a joke.

I amble around the huge store, searching for the fan gear. *Ooh, cute gym gear.* Not as cute as the outfit I last got online. Fishing, nope. Camping, nope. *Ooh, cute shoes.* I stand staring at the new pink Nikes. Okay, no more ogling shoes. *Where in the world is the rugby league section?*

As I start toward the rear of the shop, dizziness overwhelms me. The room spins. I can hear my heartbeat rushing in my ears. *Boom-ba-boom, boom-ba-ba-boom, boom-ba-ba-ba-boom, boom-ba-boom.* My back aches. The list of heart transplant rejection symptoms from the brochure runs through my head.

No, no, no, no, no, no.

I retreat between the sales racks to the left of the shoe display until I hit the wall and slide to the floor. *Is this what a transplant rejection feels like?*

"Are you okay?"

Startled, I force my head up to see a young man who would've normally taken my breath away, but I have no breath left to give. His skin is almost as dark as mine, but it's from a tan. Jet-black hair curls around his ears and the nape of his neck, framing cheekbones — sinfully high for a guy — and a strong-lined jaw. His blue eyes brim with concern.

Oh right, I'm staring and not answering his question. I tear my gaze away from his face and look down at his long-sleeve staffer shirt with the name "Ryder" pinned to his chest.

I try to speak but suck in a deep breath instead. The guy reaches out and touches my hand, bringing me back to reality. I'm on the floor in a heap in a very public place about to burst into tears. Then, my pain evaporates at the warmth of his touch. I force the sides of my mouth up a little, averting my eyes away in shame.

A small number of people crane their necks to gawk. A man in a green tie stares at me while another guy with long brown hair grins. *Jerk!* Checking out the floor is definitely a better option.

I manage to gasp, "I'll be all right in a minute."

"Do you need me to call someone for you?" Ryder crouches beside me, his voice lower than before.

I wonder what Ryder thinks about my bizarre

behavior. Illness? *Of course.* Maybe pregnancy? *Ewww.* Or a crazy chick who had a meltdown? I settle down and shake my head.

"How about a glass of water?" he asks.

I nod and he helps me to a standing position. At full height, I come up to his shoulders. He motions for me to follow with an incline of his head. We weave in silence through the racks and shoes, heading for a door at the rear of the store.

Stale, stifling air hits me as we enter the stock room. The awkward silence continues until we get to a cramped lunchroom in the far corner of the building. He leads me past a small bench and sink, cluttered with used dishes and glasses, and a tiny cupboard crammed full of staff bags. The bulging mass keeps the door from closing.

Ryder rinses a glass. "Our cold water dispenser is broken. Is tap water okay?"

"Yes," I say, twirling a ringlet through my fingers. Shifting from one leg to the other, I continue to run through the rejection symptoms in my head but none present themselves. I'm fine, nervous, but fine.

"Here, take a load off." He drags out a chair with a tattered covering and hands me the glass.

"Thanks." I put on my brightest smile and take a sip.

"Are you okay now? Are you going to pass out?" The concern on his face appears genuine.

"No, I'm better." The glass finds my mouth as I slip into autopilot. I push aside some of the magazines that litter the table.

An alluring smile greets my response. "Good. So I am Ryder," he points to his shirt with a goofy grin on his face, "and I will be your customer service assistant today." He extends a hand, palm up.

I can't help but giggle and reply, "I'm Mishca, and I'll be your customer today." I place my hand in his almost expecting him to—and wishing he would—kiss it. A warm glow flows through my body and my new heart beats faster.

"So do you faint in stores often, or was that special treatment for me?"

"No, long-time shopper, first-time fainter." I push my chin up with some foolish pride. "Not that I actually fainted."

"No offense intended," Ryder says in a hushed tone that makes me want to take the words back.

"I'm sorry. I wasn't offended. I'm new to this."

"I thought you said you were a long-time shopper." He grins wickedly at me.

"Not new at shopping, new at—" I stop short. This isn't high school anymore, and he's not one of those high school boys who get hung up about me being a virgin with a weak heart. Besides, I don't have a weak heart anymore. I have a fresh start. "Never mind."

"Are you sure you are okay? You looked upset.

Did you want to talk about it?"

"No, I'll be all right," I reply, marveling at his kindness. "It was a, ah, nothing."

"Do you need me to go to the dressing room to get your stuff?"

"The dressing room? What do you mean?" My eyebrows pinch.

"Were you not trying those on?" He gestures to my gym clothes.

"No, this is what I wore in here." I glance down at my outfit. I haven't worn it before and the small amount of sweat from my run hasn't shown on my clothes, so in his defense, it does seem like new.

"Oh, I thought you were in a black outfit when you came into the shop." Ryder's brow furrows and he grimaces. "Sorry, my mistake."

I avoid his gaze by flipping through a car magazine from the pile on the table. *Great, does he think I'm a shoplifter?*

"Odd," Ryder remarks as I turn to a page featuring the latest Ford.

"What's odd? New cars are all pretty stock standard nowadays. If you want unusual, go for the classics."

Ryder grins. "Not the car. A girl passing up a fashion magazine for a car one."

"I can like both." I cock an eyebrow, not sure whether to be offended or not. "I also like rugby league and plays," I blurt out.

"Good to know. I like movies—does that count as liking plays? They are made from screenplays, after all."

"Ah, well, they're similar. But I like movies too," I say with a grin plastered across my face.

A guy pops his head through the door way. "Hey, Ryder. You're needed out front."

"Be right there." He glances at me apologetically. "Duty calls."

I drink until the glass is empty and get up to leave. Unfortunately, queasiness takes over and I stumble. Ryder catches my arm to steady me. I should've called my emergency numbers after my episode, but for some reason I want to save face.

"Have you got a license for those legs?"

I poke out my tongue. "Yes."

"Was it off the back of a Weet-Bix packet?"

I make a mock gasp of offence. "I'm fine now. I should get going."

"Without finishing your shopping? I am your assistant, remember? Is there something I can help you with first?" Ryder gives me puppy eyes and pouts.

"Didn't they call you out there to serve other people?" I ask, not wanting to get him in trouble.

"It is fine as long as I am serving a customer. *That* is the main thing."

I press my lips together, suppressing a giggle at his formal way of speaking, not sure if he's joking around or if he's had some pompous upbringing. "Umm, okay, could you tell me where the fan gear is, please?"

The corners of his mouth reach wider into a grin that can only be described as devilish. One side of his lips seems to reach higher than the other. "I could, but would I?"

I'm dumbfounded. Asking riddles of a girl recently slumped on the floor is hardly polite. "Pardon?"

"I could tell you where the fan section is, but you should be asking, 'Would I?' "

Oh great, handsome and an English grammar dork. Not a distraction I need right now. "Um. Okay, *would* you tell me where I can find the fan gear?"

"How about a guided tour instead? That is, if you should still be shopping?" His voice has a playful ring to it.

An inexplicable urge to hold out a hand so he can lead the way comes over me, so I shove them both into my pockets. I follow his broad shoulders as he saunters off to the store floor.

"What team do you support?"

Suddenly, this present doesn't seem like such a good idea.

"Actually, it's not for me. It was going to be a present, but maybe I should get something else." For some reason I don't make a move to go.

"Oh sure. Well, then, could I help you with something else?"

I can't resist. "You could, but would you?"

Ryder lets go a small chuckle. "Would I be able to help you with your plans for tonight instead? Maybe a movie?" That devilish grin makes a comeback.

"Maybe," I say coyly, not wanting to sound too eager. Then, I remember. "Oh wait, I can't. I have plans."

"Here." He gestures to my phone and I hand it over. He puts in his number and returns it to me. "Let me know when you work out a night you are free."

I grin, but it quickly falters at the mass of missed calls and text messages from my parents. "I've got to go."

I make a hasty exit without waiting for a reply, weaving my way through the maze of sporting equipment and clothing racks.

Escaping outside, I let free a small sigh and close my eyes. The concrete wall holds me up. After three deep breaths, I call home.

About twenty minutes later, my hand is in Dad's.

"Are you okay?" he asks. I nod in response. "Are you ready to go home?"

The sound of the store door opening startles me. Ryder walks out, a bag on his shoulder. He stops midstride with a concerned expression on his face. But he looks relived that I'm okay and not alone. Dad glances between the two of us and raises an eyebrow. Ryder waves and heads to the car park.

Dad's eyes narrow at me. "Okay, spill."

"It's nothing."

"Don't tell me that was nothing. I was his age once, and I looked at your mother like that."

"He works here and helped me out."

"If you say so." He leans down and pulls me to my feet. "Mishca, we can't be there for you, if you don't let us. Life's trials are not meant to be borne alone, that's why we have family and friends."

I nod and say nothing. This is the second time this morning he's said that to me, and for the second time guilt claws at me. I haven't told him my plans for tonight.

CHAPTER 6

I DON'T KNOW HOW you can simultaneously think, *bugger* and *yippee*, but I do. I can't believe who's sitting in the group in front of me.

"No way," I murmur.

I'd chosen an adoption support group meeting on the far north side of Brisbane because I figured I was unlikely to bump into anyone I knew there. *Epic fail.* Ryder's mouth falls open when he sees me. I resist the urge to bolt out the door. He raises his hand in a casual hello.

I gulp.

An intricate weaving of tattoos snake down his arm, previously hidden under his store uniform. These aren't like the thick tribal tattoos so many guys get. Instead they're delicate and detailed, and reach down to his elbow. *Do they flow onto his chest, or back?* I try to visualize it. *How muscled is his chest and back?* Judging by his biceps, I'd say very.

A thin, pale, Goth guy, who at a guess should've been old enough to have outgrown the Goth phase, leans forward in the chair beside Ryder. He has hollowed-out cheeks, emphasizing his slender frame, and jet-black hair with a tinge of blue to it. His long fringe sweeps forward over his face, covering one green eye. He glances up and nods at me somberly. Ryder, on the other hand, beams at me, patting the spare chair on the opposite side of him. I'm late, and with no other seating choices, I scoot over.

"Well, well, well. If I had known your favorite Thursday night ritual was Adoptees 'R' Us, I would have offered to bring you here instead of a movie."

I pull a face. "Maybe it wasn't the activity. Maybe it was the company. You're not being a creeper, are you?"

Ryder clutches his *wounded* chest in mock horror, and then extends his hand. "Mishca, my heart will never be the same."

Nor will mine. He remembered my name.

As I sit down, Ryder points at Goth-guy. "This is my mate, Connor. If ever you need techno help, ask him. He has mad computer skills."

Connor rewards me with an incline of the head but says nothing.

Ryder raises an eyebrow at me. "What about you, Mishca? Where do your skills lie? Apart from being a play-loving, rugby league fan." My heart skips a bit and my stomach plunges.

Before I can speak, curvaceous lady moves to the front of the room and holds up her hand for silence. Talk about saved by the bell. My attention falters. She's wearing the highest heels I've ever seen. *Must be really short without them.* But when she opens her mouth to speak, I can't believe such a big voice can come out of such a small woman.

"Hi, I see we have some new faces tonight. I'm Sherry Tomkins, the group leader. We'll start off by introducing ourselves and perhaps outlining the reasons we're here. If you're not ready to talk about that, please at least share your name so we can call you something other than *you in the green shirt.*"

It turns out to be a mixed group, including some people who've adopted children, and others who are searching for their parents, and even some who have recently found them. Not everyone's in crisis; some have already found their happy ending and want to help others. Connor doesn't speak, just flicks his hand to pass on his turn. Ryder, I discover, is like me, trying to find his birth parents — well his mum, specifically — and I discover his last name: Madson. I can't find the courage to say anything other than my name when it comes to me.

After the introductions we have a break, which I assume is to allow some time for socializing and to give Sherry an opportunity to meet the new people. Ryder motions to follow him and Connor as they join up with a guy called Jamal, who looks part indigenous. He greets Ryder with the manly bumping of fists. Even though I'm not the single adoption group virgin tonight, Sherry starts with me.

"So Mishca," Sherry begins as we take a few steps away from the group, "did Ryder tell you about the meeting?"

I drag my gaze up from her kick-ass shoes. "No, we met today."

Sherry seems surprised but continues, "Okay. So what brings you here?"

"I want to find my birth parents."

"I see. It's not always a simple process. There are some brochures on the table. Make sure you grab one when you go. It has our counseling contacts on it. They can help you with specific search details. After the break we'll be going into smaller groups and you can pick people's brains about their journeys. Take advantage of it. I hope you enjoy the rest of the meeting." She touches my arm and heads off to the next newbie.

A girl about my age flounces over, her red hair bobbing behind her. "Hello. Trista Walsh. You enjoying your first meeting?" She loops her pale, freckly arm into mine.

"So far." I send a distress signal to Ryder with my eyes. His dance in amusement. I scowl back.

"Hey Mishca, will you come back again next

month?" Trista asks before proceeding to shove a chocolate chip muffin into her mouth.

I smile weakly.

She swallows her mouthful of muffin in a strained gulp. "You know there are meetings every night around the city?" She shoves a blue photocopied flyer into my hand.

Oh my goodness, is this girl a meetings addict?

"Haven't I seen you somewhere before?" Trista asks before finishing off her muffin.

"No, I don't think so," I say, shaking my head.

"You don't go to Infinite Energy Gym, do you? It's a few streets away from here."

"Nope," I respond.

"All right, everyone, please return to your seats," Sherry says in her rich voice.

After a quick talk from Sherry, we break off into smaller groups, and the more experienced attendees are put with the newbies. Ryder puts on the worst pretend sad face I've ever seen as we head in different directions.

I sit with Trista, my new freckled pal, and Matt Jorgensen, a parent who had been found and loves it so much he wants to help others.

I can't find any words when it's my turn. Matt breaks the silence. "Mishca, what do you know so far?" he asks in a voice you'd use to calm a skittish horse.

"Well, I was born in the United States." I pause.

Guilt twinges inside, considering Mum and Dad are under the impression I'm out with friends. They haven't noticed the lack of Mishca friend interaction since school ended last year. "I haven't been able to find any contact details for the adoption agency, and I haven't gotten a response from them at all when I made an enquiry through a form on their website." *Bastards!*

Trista edges forward. "Who's the agency?"

"Eleithyia Elite Family Services."

This strange unspoken moment passes between them. I refuse to let it slide. "What gives?"

"You're screwed. They aren't real forth—oww!" Trista receives a swift kick from Matt. She glares at him and gets a pointed stare in return. Matt catches Sherry's eye. Her heels click on the wooden floor as she makes a beeline to us. She leans in to listen to Matt, curly locks obscuring her face. His jaw sets hard.

After a second, she straightens and turns to me. "Mishca, how about you and I get some fresh air." It's not a question, so I obligingly follow. Once outside, Sherry faces me. Even in the dark, I can see her eyebrows pinching together.

"Mishca, honey, I don't know how to say this delicately, so I'm going to say it outright. You're always welcome here for support in dealing with your situation. We can help you cope and move on. But give up on your birth parents now. You won't find them."

The revelation is like being hit up the side of the head by Thor's hammer. "Why?"

"This agency...," her pause is heavy as if she's framing what she'll say in her head, "we've never traced a birth parent through *them*. I've never heard of anyone else succeeding either—only dead ends and heartache. When people throw themselves into this, it's mentally and emotionally exhausting. And when you come up empty-handed after all that effort, it can kill you inside."

I recoil but nod to show I've heard. I gulp in air. I'm...deflated. Tears well up and the dam is about to burst. I can't go inside. Sherry heads in to fetch my things, and like a zombie I go to my car, unlock the doors, and sit down. I rub my tongue against the roof of my mouth to squash the urge to break down until after Sherry leaves for good. I hate people seeing me cry. I've been weak and helpless to others for long enough. Once she has given me my things and goes, I cave into the tears.

I let out a tribal yell as a spurt of anger consumes me. *All of it.* The thought hits me absently. *Let out all of it.* When the sobs dissipate, I take some deep breaths to get ready for the drive home.

With one last sniff, I yank at the key in the ignition. The motor doesn't kick over. Dad won't be impressed. He bought me a Bufori—a rare hand-

built car — when I passed my driver's test. It's like a
Barbie gangster car, but it's a custom body on a VW
Beetle chassis. Sturdy, tough, and almost impossible
to speed in.

Mine's hot pink. Not the type of car you leave
out in Brisbane overnight. I decide to try it one
more time. Frustrated, I turn the key hard. There's a
sharp wrenching sound, and the key cracks with
half of it snapped off in the ignition.

*What the – ? That's a brand new key! There's no way
that should have happened. Am I jinxed?*

A tap at my window nearly makes me jump a
mile. My hands snap up, ready to strike, but they
relax at Ryder peering at me with that cheeky grin.

My insides twist. *Why would I do that?* I'm into
flight, not fight.

"Everything okay?" he asks.

Clearly not! I can't suppress the scowl. Ryder
raises his hands in defense.

"I heard the chug-a-lugging of a car not starting
and thought you might need a lift."

It's a much better option than explaining to my
folks what I'm doing in North Brisbane on a Friday
night instead of at the movies with friends.

"Maybe, but I shouldn't leave Betsy here."

"Betsy?" An eyebrow heads skyward. "Betsy the
Bufori?"

I'm impressed. Most people don't have a clue
about Buforis. Still, I stick out my tongue. No one

disses my Betsy.

Ryder punches numbers into his phone. "Hey, Will. Yeah, good. How about you? Hey, could you swing by for a job now? Yep. Yep. Sturt Street. A Bufori Maddison. A Bu-fo-ri. Just look for the flashy pink car. Ten minutes. Cool."

Like a gentleman, he opens my car door. "My mate Will is going to be here in ten. He will put Betsy on his car carrier and take her home. Here, give him your address." He hands me his phone.

Connor comes out and says his farewells to Ryder while I give Will the address and some thanks. I hit the end button before handing him the phone. Hope he didn't need to talk to his mate again.

Ryder leads me over to the other side of the car park. *Cool, an EH Holden.* My hours of forced participation in Dad's old car infatuation pay off. It's in immaculate condition with a metallic red paint job. All the chrome is in place too. I climb inside. The interior is even better. Custom white and candy red striped seats, a wooden steering wheel. The stereo pumps out rock music when Ryder turns the key.

The car drives like a dream. I give Ryder some very general directions. After a bit he broaches the meeting. "So you are an eefs, yeah?"

I'm not sure how to respond.

"Sorry, that was rude. We call people that come

from your agency, E E F S-eefs." When he puts it together it sounds like a shortened curse. I still can't find the energy to respond.

Suddenly, he pulls over and peers at me. "I know they told you it was hopeless, but do *not* give up. Nothing is impossible." He grabs my hand. "No one believes me, but I remember my birthmother. They said I was only six months old when she left me, but I remember her. She leant over and kissed me goodbye. Told me to be good and to not be like her, but to change and have a better life. I have never given up on her. You should not give up either."

Electricity buzzes around us, and for a second, I swear there's no oxygen left in the car. He drops my hand and shifts in his seat. I'm staring at him, my new heart pounding in my chest. Something happens between us in that quiet instant, but I can't name it. It's almost...something.

The moment passes and the atmosphere returns to normal mostly. Tiny sparks of attraction remain unspoken.

"Better get you home."

He waits for a break in the traffic, and then steers the car into the lane.

"So what else do you like to do apart from attending Adoptees 'R' Us meetings?" Ryder asks after we've driven a few blocks. "Aside from your interest in plays, rugby league, and cars, that is."

"Shopping," I reply, and then bite my lip. That sounds so shallow. "I love to read, watch movies, and I love drama."

"As in acting?"

"Yep. Love being a drama queen." I wince inwardly. Everything I say tonight seems to come out wrong.

Ryder laughs as we slow down for a red light. "I get what you mean now. I thought you meant you loved watching plays, but you want to be in them too. What have you been in so far?"

"Nothing," I reply lamely. "I took drama at school. But I was too chicken to try out for anything."

"Nothing yet," he corrects me. "Give yourself time to blossom."

He stares at me again, grinning. I return the smile as my insides twist in excitement. The red glow of the traffic signals change to green, but he keeps watching me. I want to look away. I can't. I hold his gaze. Every inch of me wants to kiss him, a very un-Mischa-like thing to do. The old Mishca anyway.

I lean in. Ryder mirrors my move.

Honk!

"Whoops," says Ryder, swiveling around to face the road. "Which way now?"

"Highgate Hill," I say. "The turnoff is still a few streets away."

He visibly stiffens and goes quiet. He's like stone by the time we reach my house.

A four-story Highgate Hill home may seem intimidating, but it isn't the response I was expecting. Most people gush all over me at first, and then try to worm so far up my ass they would never see sunlight again. Discovering a girl's got rich parents changes things, I guess.

It's a relief when we pull up in front. But I don't want it to end like this. I text him a brazen message: "Tomorrow night?"

Text messages are cute, right?

He looks up from his phone smiling, but uncertainty lingers on his face.

My phone pings. "Pick you up 2morrow at 5? Prepare 2 b scared."

I get out of the car with a grin to rival the Cheshire cat.

CHAPTER 7

AN ALL-CONSUMING *blackness engulfs me. I can't see anything. I'm lying down. A strong, sharp pain sears my chest. I try to sit up, but firm hands grasp my arms, keeping me in place. Struggling doesn't work. I'm trapped. A bright light switches on above. People dressed in black surround me. My vision adjusts slowly, revealing the group in medical garb.*

"What a horrible daughter you are." One leans in, the mouth moving under the surgical mask.

"You are betraying their trust." The second's eyes narrow at me. I stare into the black irises.

"Useless," says a third, tugging at my operating gown, "that's what you are. Useless. A good-for-nothing."

I try to protest, but the words won't come.

"Heartless." A fourth casts a shadow over me. "Yes, you are heartless. You used up your heart until it could no longer stand to beat inside your chest. Then, you stole

one from another." The fourth figure retreats and the dazzling light overhead blinds me.

Pressure pushes at my chest. I force my neck up to see a fifth black figure holding a scalpel against me. "I like heartless people." It's the familiar voice again. The hand presses the scalpel harder, breaking the skin, and blood soaks into the material against my chest. Pain explodes. "I think I will take out yours," the other hand yanks down the surgical mask to reveal rotting flesh and jagged teeth, "again."

The light gleams off the scalpel as it's raised, poised to slash open my chest.

I scream.

Darkness invades once more. I bolt upright. Smelly Belly opens an eye at me from the end of my bed, unimpressed at being disturbed. I strain my ears to listen for footsteps, but they don't come. Maybe I didn't scream out loud this time. I seriously didn't need that dream to make me feel any worse about going to the adoption meeting last night. I don't want to imagine how Mum and Dad would react if they found out.

I get up and jump in the shower, refreshed by the warm water. But when I glance down and see my scar, the dream floods my mind. I give the taps a vicious twist to cut off the flow, and then pause, inhaling. *No more breaking things.* I turn them with a gentle twist and reach for the towel. The sooner I can cover that hideous thing, the better. I throw on a pair of cutoffs and a high-necked top and head downstairs. Smelly Belly, of course, follows.

"Morning," says Dad, before taking a sip of his coffee.

"Good morning," I reply cheerily, pushing down the guilt of last night's deception. My gaze drifts to the hall. I need to check and see if Betsy made it home last night.

Smelly Belly looks put out and rubs against Dad for attention. He scratches her at the base of her tail. Her raspy pink tongue flickers. She definitely thinks she's a dog.

"Mishca, this cat is living up to her name. Time for a bath."

My nose scrunches, remembering the last time I gave her a bath and ended up covered in scratches.

"Not today, Dad. I have too much to do."

Dad's eyes narrow, sensing something afoot. "What's so important you'd neglect your furry friend?"

I smirk. Dad hates not being in the know. "I have a date."

From the lounge room I hear a thump, possibly Mum falling from Pilates first position. She peeks around the corner, and then disappears from view, before going to the fridge for a glass of water. *A rather convenient eavesdropping excuse, Mum.* She always has a water bottle beside her during workouts.

"A date, eh? Can he play rugby league?"

"That didn't come up."

"You're going to need a new dress," says Mum, her voice rising. "How about we go shopping? I'm finished anyway."

Dad nods, doing his best interpretation of a bobble head.

Mum gets ready quicker than I've ever seen before and whisks me away. In less than five minutes, we're out the door.

"Let's take Betsy. It's a great day to be driving with the top down."

"We can't," I start freaking about the possibility of my car not being here. I search for a rational excuse for my car's disappearance but can't find one.

"You parked out in the street," says Mum, pointing to my bright pink car. "You know I don't like it when you do that."

"Uh-huh," I murmur, grateful Ryder's pal came through. "There's an issue with the ignition. I'll get Dad to check on it when we get back."

Mum glances sideways at me but says nothing and heads to the garage.

The trip into Queen Street Mall is a smooth one, and before long, we're going from one dress shop to the next.

We scour the racks in the third shop, giggle, and tease each other while dresses weigh down my arms. It's a novelty that I have a guy on the scene.

But it's also so great to be spending time together without Mum stressing over my recovery.

"Hey, would you like me to put those—oh, hey, Mishca." Nerissa Murray, the *it* girl from Brighton Academy, beams at me with her arms outstretched to take my bundle of clothes. I haven't seen her since we graduated last year. With dead-straight blond hair and blue eyes that match the sea, she's more likely to be mistaken for being related to my mum than I am. I bite my lip, not needing the reminder of how different we look. "Doing some serious shopping? Let me put those in a dressing room for you."

"It's okay. I'm ready to try these on."

I slip inside and pull the curtain across. Unfortunately, sexy dresses aren't scar-friendly.

On my fifth outfit Mum pokes her head through the curtains, pulling them further apart when she sees I'm decent. She gives me an uncanny smile like she's trying to be reassuring but fails.

"How's it going?" Nerissa stops short, staring, horrified at my reflection. The scar. She recovers and fakes a bright smile. "Well, that green is your color."

The two of them step away and the curtain swings closed.

Stupid scar! Rage builds up inside me. I grip the wooden hanger for the next dress. Even though it's gone, my old heart is still causing drama. My knuckles turn white. With a crack, the hanger breaks in two.

"Is everything all right in there?" Nerissa calls. "Are you okay with sizes?"

I'm stunned at the broken wood in my hands. It takes me a few seconds to recover enough to respond. "I'm fine, thanks."

Anxiety grips my stomach and twists. *First the running. Then, the key. The other accidents. And now this. What's happening to me? Freak.*

My breathing picks up. I have to fight to get my lungs under control.

No. It's just your new heart. You were a sick weakling before. Dr. Thompson said you'd feel different, stronger.

I shove the broken hanger under a clothes rack on the way out of the dressing room.

I end up buying three outfits, partly because I like having choices and partly from the guilt about the damage to the hanger. I see one of the dresses has small splinters of wood stuck to it when Nerissa puts it in the bag. If she notices, she doesn't say anything.

CHAPTER 8

GIDDY, I TWIRL around in the lace-trimmed green baby-doll dress. It falls above my knees in a cute if a bit sassy way. The dress emphasizes the sleek lines of my legs, especially with the gold sandals I bought to match. Best of all, the high neckline hides my scar.

Ryder's widened eyes and inability to speak coherent sentences when I answer the door makes it all worth it. Mum and Dad tried to beat me to the front. Seeing as I have never brought a boy home, or even had a proper date before, I've been getting the impression my folks were starting to think I might bat for the other team — or should that be the same team? Not that it'd matter if I did, but a guy at the door is a pretty big deal for them.

I'd hoped to do the basic introductions and then make a break for it, but the three of them — even Ryder — are having no part of it. Mum ushers Ryder inside, scolding him for calling her Mrs. Richardson instead of Alicia, and prances off to get him a drink. I want the floor to open up and swallow me whole as Dad blatantly looks Ryder up and down.

At least Mum's more discreet about it. I can see from Dad's expression he's impressed, on face value anyway. Being a rugby league coach, he values athleticism and Ryder looks the part. Working at a sports store probably has certain advantages, such as a discount on weights.

"So Ryder," says Dad, "I remember seeing you at Fitness Factory downtown. Is this a permanent career?"

Ah, Dad, so not subtle. It's a first date and they're mapping out whether he's a potential father for their grandchildren.

"No, I will drop back to casual next year when I start university."

"Oh, university, what are you studying?" Mum returns with a glass of Coke for Ryder.

He gives his thanks, takes a sip, and then places it on the table before responding. "Environmental law."

Cha-ching! Score points for Ryder.

"Oh, really? And what school were you at this year?" Dad asks.

"Well, I put off uni so I could work for a couple of years and save to pay for my studies."

"Oh, so that makes you three years older than

Mishca?" Mum fishes for information.

Dad clears his throat. "You're twenty-one?"

"Yes, sir." Ryder meets my dad's eyes as he says it.

I want to staple Dad's lips together. *Three years? Big deal!* And that's enough of a Ryder grilling for me. I pull at Ryder's arm before Dad can blurt out another irrelevant question. "Okay, time for us to go."

When we're out the door, I glance at Ryder to make sure my parents haven't scared him off. He grins at me like a goofball, so I'm taking that as he's still interested.

"Are you still going to come to the support meetings?" asks Ryder as he opens the car door for me. "You did become the highlight of the evening."

"I'm not sure." I grin. "Even if I can't find my parents through the support group, there may be other benefits of attending."

"Benefits are good." Ryder's lips pull even wider. He starts up the car and the motor purrs. "Ready?"

"As I'll ever be."

Time for a new me in every way.

* * * *

It's a long drive to Inala. We pull onto the driveway of a very old house. *No wonder he felt uncomfortable dropping me off.* The white house has paint peeling off to reveal sections of grey. A small gravel driveway leads through to a brand new shed at the back. It stands out against the state of the house, but I figure it's where Ryder keeps his car safe from vandals and thieves.

We make our way through and park in the shed. *Called it.* The house has no fly screens, and the windows are a mix of louvers and wooden-framed push outs. We have only a couple of steps to walk up to get to the back door. Inside is immaculate. It's deceptive, given the outside. I wonder if Ryder did the renovations himself. Suddenly, an image of Ryder painting hits me, shirt off with splatters of paint over a ripped body. I almost start drooling. *Embarrassing.*

"I hope you are ready for some scary stuff. We are doing a classic thriller movie-fest night," Ryder informs me as he leads me into the lounge room. "Sorry, there were no movie adaptions of plays. All picked out a few days ago."

I thought it'd be the two of us, so I stop in my tracks at the sight of someone else in the room. Before me stands the most amazing creature I've ever seen. My shoulders hunch, as though making myself smaller will allow me to blend into the wall. I'm a grandma frump in my smock compared to this one.

The setting sun spills onto her shockingly blue-green hair. It glimmers like an emerald in the light.

The fringe is cut in a blunt diagonal with the remainder falling straight down to her waist like some sort of perfect Fae creature. Her skin shines as smooth as porcelain, and her eyes match her hair. They are the same shape as Ryder's, creating a glorious yin and yang pair. Similar in shape and aura, yet opposites like light and dark.

His sister? I hang on to the smidge of hope.

Her eyes lock with mine and they give off one vibe—rival.

Nope, not a sibling.

She turns away to stare out the window without a word, and her hands seem to clench at her sides. *Crud!* She's beating me in the bosom stakes. My average C cups seem like nubs. I can't even guess at her size, but it's impressive. Tight black leggings hemmed with lace hug her legs. A purple and black striped top fits snug against her, a second skin on her slender frame. I can't pin down the look. *Not Emo and not Goth. Definitely alternative, though.*

Ryder clears his voice. "Sophitia, this is Mishca."

She raises a carefully shaped eyebrow. "Charming to meet you, Miss Mishca. I gather you will be joining us tonight?" Her voice reminds me of smooth caramel. The words seem to glide out of her mouth and melt into my mind. She has a regal air. Something about the way she talks reminds me of Ryder.

I smile uncertainly in response. Sensing my

discomfort, Ryder squeezes my hand. The tension breaks when Connor enters the room with pizza and drinks. *Is this a double date?* I doubt he's here at this time of night to fix Ryder's computer.

"Hey man, you made it. Taken down any evil corporations this week through cyber warfare?" Ryder asks with a straight face and laughing eyes. They do that manly, brotherly slapping thing, though Connor seems much less enthusiastic about it than Ryder. *I don't get guys.*

My gaze sweeps the room. Mismatched lounges, including a two-seater beanbag and an entertainment system befitting a bachelor pad take up key positions. A small bookshelf catches my attention. Nestled in the corner of the shelf, a tiny metal photo frame rests.

"Who's this?" I ask, pointing to the soldier in the picture. He has brown hair and eyes with a solid jaw and a large Roman nose. No family resemblance to Ryder.

"That is my roommate's dad."

"Oh." I put it down like he'd told me it was contagious.

As we're about to sit, a knock at the door sends Ryder ducking off. He introduces Perdita, who everyone calls Perdi, and her boyfriend, Steven. They both work with Ryder. Their slight but muscular frames indicate they probably take advantage of the discounts at the Fitness Factor too.

Perdi has waist-length brown hair I've longed for all my life. Anything to have my appearance a bit more like Mum's. Jamal and Trista, from the adoption meeting, follow them in.

We fill the small lounge room. Perdi and Steven snavel the three-seater lounge; although they have to shuffle over to let Trista in. Connor has commandeered the armchair, much to the disappointment of Jamal who gets plain old floor, while Ryder and I take the giant two-seater beanbag. Sophitia stands in the doorway.

We finish a superhero movie and are about to put on a thriller when Ryder decrees we should stop for a refreshment break. I turn to meet Sophitia's hard gaze as I grab a glass of water. Connor has also made his way through the maze of bodies to the kitchen.

"Did you enjoy it?" I ask, hoping I can connect with at least one of Ryder's friends.

He faces me with a deadpan look. "Yes, I did. I've seen it five times now. The concept of everyday people being hidden heroes in a more realistic context is believable and worthy of research."

Whoa! Okay.

We talk a little more about the movie until the opening credits of the new one start and someone's yelling from the lounge room about moving our butts. Poor Connor has lost his seat to Jamal, but he opts to retrieve two bar stools from the dining room and offers one to Sophitia.

Not long into the movie Ryder yawns, stretches, and places his arm around me. I shoot him a sarcastic *you're so smooth* look. He simply shrugs and grins in response, pulling me closer to him.

We have another mandatory break before we start on the next film. Ryder leads me outside to the patio where a hammock hangs between two poles. We work our way into it. I inhale his scent and snuggle closer. He smells like cedar wood, musk and something spicy I can't put my finger on. His warmth envelops me like a security blanket, pushing away any doubts I have about competing with Sophitia for his attention. I dangle one arm over the side of the hammock, relishing the light evening breeze.

"Are you enjoying the madness of Madson Mansion?"

I can't tell if I'm meant to read anything into that last part considering how small his place is. I hope it's not a jab at my family, but I roll with it. "Sure, I love being a sardine." I poke him in the ribs. "Nah, it's been fun. I like thrillers and it's good you're not afraid to introduce me to your friends."

"Well, actually, you are yet to meet the one you have to impress."

I suppress a giggle. "Uh huh? Would this be your gal pal that you've known since you were three and shared naked romps with in the backyard?"

"I wish I could boast of naked backyard romps with a gal pal, but sadly, no. It is Finlay, but do not call him that unless you want him to shoot me death stares all night." He smiles. "On second thought, call him that. It will be hilarious."

His formal way of speaking sets off electric sparks inside. It's struck me before, but seems even more pronounced now. I haven't heard the guy use a contraction in the short time I've known him. *Weird for a grammar nerd.* I contemplate calling him on it, but I don't want to ruin any chance of romance. And he's so charming. Like a prince pretending to be a pauper.

Ryder doesn't expand on the topic of Finlay's name, despite my best efforts. He tells me that they met in grade two, fought over a football, wrestled, punched and kicked each other, and have been best friends ever since.

I fall into an awkward silence, mulling over the fact I have no Finlay. Dad took different coaching jobs, moving us around until we settled in Brisbane. I ended up like a satellite, circling around groups and trying to work out where I fit. When I finally found some steady friends, I was still on the outer edges, looking in, wishing I was part of the inner sanctum. No surprise I haven't heard much from them since they left for Europe. Before I can sink into a melancholy funk, something cold and wet attacks my dangling hand. I yelp. A lopsided mouth pants back. The lolling tongue of a grunting dog — a staffy — begs for pats.

"Hey Jelly Roll, stop trying to scare Mishca." I love it when he says my name.

Sophitia's head appears from the entry, all gorgeous despite the scowl on her face. "We are starting, with or without you two."

Well, excuse me.

We work our way out of the hammock and inside the house. Of course, we've lost our beanbag. Ryder leans against the doorframe, wrapping his arms around me. He presses me against him so tight that I'm very aware of the contours of his body. *Definitely a set of abs under there.* I inhale and imagine being surrounded by his scent while kissing him. Unfortunately, standing like that isn't ideal for too long, and the desire for a comfortable seat takes over.

Somehow, Trista, Connor, and Jamal have commandeered lounge seating, so Ryder pulls rank and makes Connor and Jamal move.

Near the end of the movie I hear footsteps behind us.

Pace indicates casualness, not an attack. No threat. The thought flies through my brain like credits on the screen before I can read into it. *What?*

I shake my head to clear the insane thoughts; then, I peek over my shoulder to see a young man propped on a barstool. He has a strong profile with a patrician nose, thin lips, and a broad jaw. Not as tall as Ryder, he's still about six foot but broader and even more muscular. *Mr. Finlay, I presume.* He glances over at me with an unreadable expression, and then returns his attention to the movie.

As the credits roll, I check my watch and see I'm going to turn into a pumpkin if we don't leave soon. Ryder and I say our goodbyes and head to the shed. I open the passenger door and slide into the seat. Before I can close the door, a hand holds it open. Finlay peers in and smirks.

"Hello Ryder's date, whom I've so rudely not been introduced to yet. Do you mind if I tag along for the ride? I haven't seen my boy all week."

I glance at my date, who shoots daggers at his BF. Unable to catch Ryder's eye, I inch along the bench seat until I get to the gear stick, which unfortunately, has been modified off the column and onto the floor. I raise my leg up and over, my dress swishing and showing more of me than I would have preferred. My face burns as Finlay appreciates the display. Ryder, who is not receiving the full show from the driver's seat, isn't too happy with Finlay's front-row view.

"Fin, this is Mishca. Mishca, this is Fin," says Ryder. "We were not expecting you home until tomorrow."

Ryder reaches down between my knees and

jams the gears into reverse.

"Me neither, but the plan changed." Finlay puts on a mock-offended tone. "You weren't trying to avoid me? Am I that much of an embarrassment that you didn't want me meeting Mishca?"

Ryder reaches again and puts the car into first. "Whatever would give you that idea? It is not like you would ever do anything to embarrass me."

His hands are there again, racing through the gears. Not quite how I'd expected the scene playing out the first time a guy's hands traveled between my thighs. *Hello awkward.*

We ride in silence until I'm itching with anticipation.

"So Fin. I can call you Fin, can't I? Were you that desperate to spend time with your mate, or did you want to scope me out to see if I'm good enough?" I let the words run amok and so want to shove them back in my mouth. I have a bad habit of speaking before I think.

"What if I said a little bit from column A and a little bit from column B?"

"I'd say fair enough." Finlay grins at my response, and I gather I've scored a point somehow.

After a shift change, Ryder lets his hand rest on my thigh. My whole body tingles in response until I catch Finlay watching. *Typical guy!* A horrible thought flashes into my head. *I hope they don't share!* Ryder must notice because his hand returns to the steering wheel.

When we pull onto my street, Finlay gives Ryder an odd look. The porch light gleams a beacon of welcome, anticipating my return. I exit through the driver's door—a safer option to minimize flashing. At the top step, I tip my face up to Ryder, loving those soulful eyes. He reaches his hand to my chin and brings his lips to mine for a brief gentle kiss. Sparks zip around in my stomach.

"Could I see you again tomorrow?"

"You could," I smirk, "but will you?"

"Yes, I will. How about I pick you up around eight and we go into the city to check out the nightlife?"

I nod and pause, hoping for another kiss. Instead, Ryder retreats down the stairs, maintaining eye contact. An impressive feat, backwards and all. He turns and saunters down the path, hands in his pockets. He stops at the gate and gives me a smoldering gaze that sends electric tingles all over. I slide my key into the door and open it, but I watch until his car is out of sight. *Out of sight but not out of mind.* I'm sure I will dream of Ryder tonight. At least, I hope I will.

* * * *

In a cave I can hear the ocean waves lapping against rocks. The sunlight beckons me, as does Ryder. He calls to me. Happiness radiates in his voice. I try to move but find my feet and hands are shackled to a wall. I want to call to him, yet my voice stays silent. A malignant presence swamps me, suffocating me with fear, despair, and guilt.

A familiar man with long brown hair appears to my right. "Let me help you, Mishca." I know him. He's the owner of the voice that has haunted my dreams.

My chest tightens. The presence steps forward, draped in a large cloak. Bone-thin hands reach in and pull something from the inner folds.

The man speaks to me again. "Come to me. It is the only way."

I see something glimmer in the darkness. He moves toward me and slashes at my face – with a feather duster?

I spring to consciousness to find Smelly Belly purring on my chest, her tail flipping over my face. A half sneeze escapes me. Cat hair flies up my nose. I scan the darkness for threats, half expecting to see a figure with skeletal hands hidden in the shadows.

Nothing.

I make out the edges of my furniture, the doorframe, and my computer. No cloaked figures. Yet an uneasy feeling takes hold. I close my eyes in case I can hear anything my vision couldn't detect. Even though I know for certain no one is in the room with me, I can't stop hearing the voice in the dark. My eyelids snap open, and I stare at the ceiling with the knowledge that sleep is an impossible dream.

CHAPTER 9

A SEA OF GYRATING bodies surrounds Ryder and me, whooping it up to the latest remixed tracks. Nerissa Murray waves from nearby. Selling me a dress has made us fast friends. Not that I'm complaining. The Bowl is the hottest nightspot in Brisbane, and Nerissa's uncle happens to own it. My new connection invited us to their private booth and scored discount drinks. I can't indulge after my operation. But still cool.

Blue glass features cover every inch of space. Where glass isn't practical, there's wood. The main attraction houses five dome VIP rooms that aren't exactly private. Off to the side of the dance floor, a DJ listens to some women, probably requesting a song. I lace my fingers through Ryder's and let him lead me over to the private booth.

"Would you like a drink?" Ryder yells over the music. I frown. His voice sounds so loud even over the pumping bass. *Weird.* He must take it as I can't hear him, so he leans in and repeats his question. His warm breath caresses my skin, and yet I shiver a little.

"Sure, if you're buying." I try my best for sultry, but I'm not sure if I pull it off. "But just water."

"Huh?'

"Just a water," I repeat louder, but I still don't know if he hears me.

I enjoy watching him saunter over to the bar. The boy's got swag.

He makes his way through the crowd with two drinks in hand. I haven't warned him about my condition, not wanting to scare him off. If he knew I had a heart transplant, it would be back into the fragile box.

But you're not fragile anymore. My mind rebels. *You can break things, run fast, and now you can hear someone like nothing in a crowded room filled with music.*

Shut up! I bite my lip and try my best to push away the little voice in my head. How do I know this isn't normal seeing as I've never been normal before?

Then, why haven't you spoken to Dr. Thompson about any of this in your checkups?

I don't bother answering the wayward thoughts this time. I focus on Ryder instead. He manages to get halfway across when a pair of long pallid arms wrap around his waist. Sophitia snares him, pressing against his back, but her eyes laser on me. They blaze hot as hellfire as the strobe lights flash. Her long green hair falls over Ryder's shoulder. She whispers in his ear, her gaze still locked with mine. She removes one arm from his chest and snakes it toward the glass. She winks at me as she snags the drink and makes a gnashing gesture with her teeth.

Yes, you're all woman and could eat him up at any time.

Ryder's gaze flicks between me and Sophitia; then, he hands me his orange juice, which escapes Sophitia's clutches.

"Exactly what I felt like."

His creased brow evens at my reply.

Conversation is hard with the noise—I can hear Ryder, but he can't hear me. It doesn't matter. I'm in no mood for talking. I'm too busy playing out the various scenarios in my mind for how things could go down tonight.

Ryder keeps sneaking glimpses at me in a shy way.

"Want to share?" I ask, offering him the last of the orange juice.

Before he can answer, Finlay plonks down on the seat next to us. He doesn't speak to me again after an initial nod and "Hey." His third wheel status doesn't seem to bother him one bit as he bops in his seat to the throbbing music.

Ryder, on the other hand, frowns. Still the chair

dancing is infectious, and I join in. I'd like to think my mad skills at seated dancing inspire Ryder to get me onto the dance floor, but whatever the reason, I don't protest when he grabs my hand and tugs me up.

The music pulses through me. I lean into Ryder, moving against him to the beat. His hand presses into the small of my back, keeping our hips interlocked. I reach my arms around Ryder's neck, and he moves in. His lips brush against mine. Sparks ignite where ever our skin touches and it's on. Ryder's tongue runs across my lower lip then pushes deeper into my mouth. My body goes on autopilot and responds. I press myself against him, moving to our own rhythm that has nothing to do with the beats.

Finally, we come up for air. He gazes at me, breaking into a full blown smile. Nerissa, dancing close by, glances at me over her boyfriend's shoulder and gives me a thumbs-up. It's perfect. As the baseline continues to pump the rhythms, I let go and the music takes over.

We stay in the throng for about an hour until Nerissa comes over and grabs my hand, pulling me in the direction of the bathrooms. At last, the music isn't at a deafening level; although, I've still got a ringing in my ear. The restrooms are as elaborate as outside. Mural mermaids cover the walls while a silver-tiled water feature rests in the corner.

Nerissa squeals, "That guy you're with is so hot, and you two look so good together."

"It's going really well. But I'm not sure if I should leave Ryder alone for too long. Sophitia might get her claws into him." I check my makeup in the mirror.

"That girl with green hair? Yeah, what's her deal?" Nerissa pumps some quick-dry sanitizer and rubs her hands together.

I shrug, concentrating on touching up my lipstick. "I dunno. I don't think she likes me very much. So where are the others tonight?" I ask, referring to her twin, Dorian, and their friends. Six of them, including Nerissa and her brother, were inseparable in high school.

It's her turn to shrug. "Family stuff. Pretty boring."

We make our way past the bathroom line and out the door. The music puts the conversation to a halt. Ryder's strong arms wrap around me and the dancing marathon starts again. An endless battery of energy flows through me, but Ryder shows signs of fatigue.

He starts walking backwards from the dance floor, coaxing me with him until we're hidden in a small corner of the club near the pool tables. He pushes me against the wall and cups my face with one hand, letting the other trail down my neck and arm as he kisses me. His hand slides from my face and presses lightly on my collarbone and neck. I freeze, worried he'll reach my scar.

He pulls away, his breathing ragged. The light catches his eyes. They glow purple under the neon.

"You are so beautiful."

He grins that grin that makes my heart flip. He moves in again but not to my lips or mouth. He nibbles on my ear, and then works his way down my neck. *Oh, please don't leave a hickey.* My body yields to the sensation of his lips against my skin. I don't want him to stop, despite the worry. The temperature around us rises.

His hand has been clutching my wrist, but now it brushes my hip and starts up my shirt. His fingers are electric against my bare skin. But I pull away a little and push his hand aside. As good as it feels, it's too fast.

Ryder presses pause as though we're already in sync. He sweeps some stray hairs from my cheek. "You look like you are ready for me to take you home," he stumbles on his words, "I mean to your home."

* * * *

We drive in silence. A nagging impression I've done something wrong consumes me. I replay the night over and over in my head, at times substituting Sophitia instead of me. I bet she would have kept the party going.

Ahhh!

I struggle not to let out a scream.

When we finally pull up, Ryder turns to me. "I am so sorry. I do not want you to be scared off. I really like you, Mishca."

A breath of relief hisses between my teeth. *Wow!*

"I really like you too, Ryder." I love saying his name. I squirm in my seat. I know I can't avoid my secret anymore.

"There's something I should tell you. Well, two things." *Okay, easy one first.* I take a breath. "I'm not very, oh, how do I put this..." *Say it.* "Well, experienced. Before this, it was just kissing. Which leads me to the next thing."

I can see Ryder's mind racing. No words come, so I decide to show him. I pull my top over my head and sit before him in my skirt with my scar and bra. The shock on Ryder's face compounds when a firm hand opens the driver's side door and yanks him from the car.

"Get your hands off my daughter."

I race out, grappling with my top, and continue around the car to pull Dad off Ryder. I shout at my father, even though Dad has opted to throw my date to the ground instead of pummeling him. I turn pleadingly to Mum, who has also appeared from nowhere.

"Make yourself decent." Dad spits the words at me.

"He didn't touch me, Dad! I was showing him my scar."

Dad, brought up short, glares. Mum puts a hand on his shoulder.

"She's serious, Tom. Come inside."

Dad spins around and stomps into the house. Mum follows him with an apologetic look.

I focus my attention on Ryder. "I'm so sorry about Dad. I thought it would be easier to show you my scar than explain."

"Scar?" says Ryder straight-faced. "What scar? I only saw a pair of beautiful breasts."

I hit him with my handbag. He laughs until I hit him again. Once I'm satisfied he's suffered enough for the breasts comment, I hand him an unused but scrunched-up tissue from my clutch to clean his face.

"So," Ryder begins, his gaze flicking skywards, "were you in an accident?"

I shake my head and watch the curiosity rising in his eyes. "A heart transplant."

"Really? Sorry that was not...um okay...wow...when?"

I give him the abridged version, hoping he isn't going be turned off by a girl who has someone else's heart beating in her chest.

"Ah dang," Ryder says at last. "Now that scar I got on my butt loses the number one 'scar story' spot." He flashes me that cheeky grin. "But I guess seeing as we are sharing war stories…" He begins to unbuckle his belt.

I stand in front of him and place my hands atop his to prevent further belt removal. He takes advantage, brushing his lips against mine, and then saunters to his car. "I'll call you. Let me know when it is safe to show my face around here again."

I wave goodbye and brace myself for whatever carnage lays inside. I open the door a crack, peering inside. Silence greets me. I push it a bit wider and poke my head in. Crisis averted. Mum already sent Dad to the guest bedroom. She waits at the kitchen table with a cup of hot chocolate. Although every inch of me wants to run past and into my room, I oblige her.

"Honey, I'm so sorry. Your dad forgets what it's like to be young. He also forgets what he and I were doing in the pool when his parents unexpectedly came home early…no wait, that wasn't your father, that was Paul Sherman."

I resist the urge to slap my hands over my ears. I so do not want to picture Mum that way. And with the sheltered upbringing I was given, I never thought of her with anyone but Dad.

"Well, your dad forgets about when he and Charmayne Pattsy were…" She trails off, thankfully. I don't need details what my father did with another woman either.

She clears her throat. "Anyway, you're young

and you have, um, hormones like any other young adult. I'm trying to say 'be safe' and all that." She pauses, and then adds, "Did you have to take your shirt off in his car?"

"I was showing him my scar. I didn't know how to tell him. I was worried he'd be freaked out." I twist my fingers in the hem of my top. Dad better not have scared Ryder off.

Mum raises a sculpted eyebrow. "Well, I think he liked what he saw, so I doubt he'll be going anywhere."

"Mum!"

"Next time, try charades or hangman instead of show-and-tell." She hops up, gives me a kiss goodnight, and heads to the guest bedroom. Dad might get a reprieve. Time to retreat to my room just in case.

Smelly Belly has made a home on my bed. Tufts of white fluff are scattered across the covers. I sit beside her, scratching her chin and letting her purring therapy relax me.

"Hello beautiful Smelly Belly." She's always dependable when I need a friendly furry face around. I change into my PJs, slip under the sheet, and kick the covers aside. Laying in my usual fetal position allows her to slip against my stomach. But I can't get to sleep. My head has too much going on inside.

I go through the list of things that have changed

about me since my operation. I reach over to my
desk, grab my laptop, and Google "super speed
strength hearing." It's a longshot, but what the
heck. All the posts on the first few pages are about
superheroes and most of them refer to Superman. I
may be adopted, but I'm not some alien that's been
taken in, so it's no help at all. Besides, I was normal
before the operation. Well, as normal as a girl with a
hole in her heart can be.

Tears threaten. I blink them away. I don't trust
myself to tell anyone about this. My parents would
spaz out, and my new boyfriend wouldn't want
anything to do with me. Any chance of a friendship
with Nerssia would be nixed. I need to keep my
head down and stop breaking things.

Smelly Belly sniffs at my fingers and plops her
head down. I give her fur some pats and try to
empty my head. Her soft rhythmic purring doesn't
quell my anxiety. Not wanting to face those dreams
that will come with sleep, I slip out of bed to get
some fresh air.

The sound of lapping water from the river
provides a constant soundtrack to the night as I
stand at the edge of the pool area. Despite the
warmth of the evening, I wrap my arms around my
midsection as a shiver convulses through my body.
Then, something else takes over. Rage surges in my
veins.

Why me? What is happening to me?

I pick up a large pot plant and hurl it over the edge. It smashes on the boat ramp below in a series of rapid-fire cracks. I stalk back inside before I do any more damage.

CHAPTER 10

RYDER RESTS HIS HEAD on my shoulder and nibbles my earlobe as I try to focus on the screen.

"You're not helping, you know," I say with a giggle.

He traces the edge of my ear with his tongue, making me squirm, and then kisses my temple. "You have nothing to worry about. I am sure your drama audition was fantastic. And worst case scenario, we study law together."

I purse my lips and twitch them back and forth, contemplating what else to choose. *Why didn't I do this last year?* My old heart still causes issues even now. I didn't see the point of applying for uni last year when I knew I would already be having a year off. My recovery time if the transplant came through, and if it didn't, well...there would have been no use in applying to school. I guess, in hindsight, it was a poor excuse. I used my heart as a crutch to avoid so much. Knowing my life was on hold, I shut down, sulked, and missed the admissions deadline.

I got my application in by the September 30th date, but I didn't complete it. Now, I've got until early January to change my preferences. I originally put law on top to keep Dad happy, but next year is about me.

Drama – choice one, tick. Law – choices two, three and four, tick, tick, tick. I'll happily let him believe the first three choices on my application are to three different universities for law. Not sure how I'll explain that when I get into the acting course, but future Mishca can worry about it.

"What about this course?" Ryder points to an Arts Degree. "You can still study drama as a major."

I scan the blurb. "Only the theory side of things." My lips tighten at the thought of Dad's reaction to that degree. I chew on it a minute, and then enter in the code. It's not like it matters. My marks should be good enough to get me into law, even if I bombed my audition for drama.

The tension in my chest releases like a helium balloon let loose into the atmosphere. *Done. No going back now.* I close the laptop with a sense of finality and step away from the table. Ryder pulls me into a hug and squeezes tight. I sink into him, our bodies connecting as if made for each other.

Ryder's phone vibrates and interrupts our blissful moment. I straighten so as not to fall on my arse as Ryder answers the call.

"Hello, Ryder speaking." I smirk at his politeness. He pauses to let the other person talk. "Sorry, I am at my girlfriend's place."

Delight squirms from my heart to the pit of my stomach like a little fairy doing a happy dance inside. I love hearing him refer to me that way — his girlfriend. We totally bypassed the whole awkward conversation about relationship status. After a couple of weeks of dates I was his girl, period.

"Hang on, I will talk you through it." Ryder mouths an apology and indicates it's work. He starts taking the person on the other end of the line through the operating procedure of some piece of gym equipment.

I smile and nod, and then walk to the pool deck, not wanting to wait around like a shag on a rock while Ryder talks shop. The sunlight bounces off the pool's surface, glinting as though covered with specks of gold. The past three weeks have been amazing, everything that I'd been hoping for: new heart, new lease on life, and new romance. Happiness plays across my lips, tugging at the corners of my mouth. I let out a contented sigh.

Sweat trickles down my brow. *Yuck.* It's still spring, but the Australian sun has been making its presence known. Another month of hot weather will be followed by two more months of sweltering to go. The oppressive heat doesn't stick to the seasons. It's hot in spring *and* autumn. What I wouldn't give for a white Christmas rather than the summer heat wave. I'd love to make snow angels and open up the presents while sipping hot cocoa. Instead, we bunker down in the air condition or cool off in the pool. Mind you, a shirtless Ryder by the pool at Christmas could be the best present of all.

Danger! I stiffen and listen. Soft footfalls, like someone trying to ambush me from behind. That now familiar tingling sensation tugs at my toes then travels up my body. Firm hands grasp my shoulders. My head jerks back, head-butting my assailant in the nose. The oath that escapes his lips does nothing to slow me down. *Male.* I reach up and grip the fingers tugging on my right shoulder, push out my hip, and fling the attacker onto the concrete. I follow up, moving in for a groin strike to disable.

A sinking realization hits me a second before I land the blow. I can't stop in time, but I don't strike with the initial intended ferocity.

"Ryder!" I kneel beside him. My hands flutter over his body as though they can sense any injury I've caused.

"You have a great self-defense teacher," he says with a wheeze.

I neglect to correct him. "Are you okay?" *Crap!*

The second I start feeling comfortable, my freakishness resurfaces. *Where did that even come from?* I rub the side of my temple, trying to shake away the weirdness. *Stay alert. You have to stay alert.*

A laugh taunts me. I close my eyes and focus. *Rooftop.* Something else takes over me. I stride away from Ryder, three long steps, and propel at the cement sidewall. My foot hits hard. I pivot, pushing toward the top of the adjacent wall that barricades our back yard.

"Mishca?" I freeze and turn back to Ryder, who has propped himself up into a sitting position. "You are putting me to shame with your wicked martial arts skills, very Jackie Chan-like, but what is going on?"

Crazy Mishca. What is going on? That laughter accompanies the words. I can't tell if the voice comes from my head or goes with the retreating footsteps I swear I can hear.

"I don't know." I groan and sit on top of the wall.

Ryder gets up with a wince and comes over to me. He tilts his head so he can look into my eyes, placing his hands on my thighs. "I know we are just starting out and trust needs to be earned, but if this relationship is going to cause me regular bodily harm, it is something I need to know about." The serious glint in his eyes betrays the light tone of his voice.

I gulp. *Do I tell him? That I break things? That I hear things? That I can outrun my dad? That I think I'm going insane because of my medication?* Anxiety crawls up my back like a hideously hairy spider. I open my mouth to say something, anything. Then, snap it shut. *No. You'll lose him.*

I opt for a half-truth. "My medication, the ones I take to make sure the transplant takes, they have side effects."

"They turn you into Wonder Woman?"

I snort, but the analogy doesn't feel all that far off. "Yes, and I keep my invisible plane in the driveway."

"So that is what I bumped into the other day."

My mouth twists. Ryder's thumb strokes the top of my thigh in a lazy circle. He cocks his head in anticipation of further explanation.

The truth will set you free...yeah right. "They give me hallucinations," I say, unwilling to divulge all my changes, especially not ones that will send him running for the hills. Ryder reaches for my hands and pulls me to him, enclosing me in his arms. "I get a bit jumpy. It's hard to explain."

Liar. You know there's more to it than that. The voice seems to float across my mind from the same spot as before. I squeeze my eyes shut and sink further into Ryder's embrace, my head against his chest. The sound of his heart beating as steady as a metronome calms me.

"Everybody has things going on in their life, Mishca." He slides his fingertips down my arms, holds my hand, and leads me over to the edge of the balcony, pointing to the river below. "It is like the river. We see the shiny surface of the water like we see people's façades. It is not until you get close to someone that you get to see what is underneath. I expected you to be like a river with lots of activity happening under the surface, not a puddle with a reflection of everything around it and no substance of its own."

"Did you just say I'm deep?" My heart starts to beat faster again, but in a way that sends pulses over my body.

"Something like that." Ryder caresses my face. His lips find mine in a brief, but nevertheless electrifying kiss. "I knew when I met you that your life was complicated. That does not scare me off. Tell me more when you are ready, and I will do the same."

"You have secrets?" I ask.

Instead of answering, he kisses me deeply, as though he's silently telling me everything I need to know, and my lips can heal whatever pain he has inside. It's enough for me.

CHAPTER 11

WHO ARE YOU? I can't be sure if I say it aloud or think it, but something echoes around my mind like bats chittering in a cave. *I'm you.*

Ugh, another dream. Not the best way to start Christmas Day. *Why won't they go away?* That man featured in my dream again. Maybe I wouldn't dream like this if I was sleeping in Ryder's arms. *Fat chance.* No way Dad would ever let him spend the night in my room. Not that I'm ready for that...yet. Thankfully, my boyfriend is very understanding and patient.

I don't know why Ryder isn't spending Christmas day with his parents, but he said he'd be over around ten. He doesn't speak much about his adoptive parents, and after he fobbed off a few probing questions, I thought it best to drop it. Maybe he's concerned about the social status gap.

I pause at the bathroom on my way out, spotting

Mum as she inspects her latest wrinkles—not that she has many. Her large array of creams has seen to that, but she can't avoid crow's feet forever. She lets loose a small sigh, turning from the mirror. When she sees me, she gives me a smile. I'm so excited that I wish her, "Merry Christmas," and dash out front to wait.

I head onto the footpath and eye Ryder's car, minus him. I walk down the street, trying to find my boyfriend. As I turn around to go home, I see him in my peripheral vision.

I stop, dumbfounded, realizing he's coming from one of the riverfront homes further down the street.

What the— A thin bald man with broad shoulders and an older woman with short curly hair follow him. Both appear to be in their early sixties.

The man clasps a friendly grip on Ryder's shoulder and shakes his hand with the free one. Ryder turns to the woman and kisses her. She takes the opportunity to squeeze him tight. When she lets go, Ryder leaves, pausing to wave. I wish I could hear what they're saying. I focus all my energy on them.

"Bye," Ryder says, spinning around one last time.

"Visit again soon," the woman replies.

My eyebrows pinch forward as I assess the couple.

No threat detected. The random thought flashes in my mind like some freaky artificial intelligence.

Wait, no threat? What the heck am I thinking? And how did I hear that from five houses away?

I inhale and expel all the breath from my lungs, trying to calm down. Today is meant to be a good day. I won't let my weirdness spoil it.

Ryder heads toward me, focusing on the pavement as though lost in thought. *You are so busted.* I have no idea what I've busted him doing, but he is. He's covered half the distance between us when he raises his face and spots me. He hesitates before continuing. The corner of his mouth twitches like he wants to smile but isn't sure if it's appropriate. He raises an eyebrow and decides it's okay to give me a grin.

"Hey, you. Merry Christmas."

"Merry Christmas to you too," I say, ignoring the voice in the corner of my head calling me a *freak*, and the other part that says *hypocrite* because I have so many secrets unshared.

There's a pause. I can see he's searching for the right words.

"So who are they?" I ask, not prepared to wait.

"Um, okay. I have found it a problem in the past...so...and...well, um. Boy, I wish I had some fun visual aids like you." I blush remembering how brash I had been stripping my top off to show him my scar. "Those are my parents."

"Oh." My voice and brain fail to produce any more words.

"Not my birth parents, but my parents who raised me. They bought that place earlier this year."

I inhale, trying to work out why Ryder waited three months to tell me this. I can't believe he didn't trust me with it. I twitch my lips at the thought. I'm keeping a lot from him too. But his secret is nothing like mine.

"So why the secrecy? Why not be upfront about it?"

Ryder's face contorts like he's in pain but then relaxes. He takes a deep breath too. "Look, just because my parents are bigwigs in the mining industry and can afford to buy every property on this street does not mean that is who I am."

Something in his tone makes my hand find his. Slowly, we make our way to my house. And here I was worried he'd be intimidated by *my* family.

Now you only have to worry about him finding out you're morphing into some crazy mutant after having a heart transplant.

Ryder takes a deep breath. "My parents and I had a falling out. They wanted me to join the family business and I have a problem with making money by raping the earth and adding to environmental problems. So after some huffing and puffing and chest thumping by my father, I moved out. It was his way or the highway, and I chose the highway.

That was about two years ago. Neither of us is willing to back down. I had to put off my studies for a while. We are just now starting to patch things up."

Some of it resonates with me, given my past experiences with fake friends. But his words leave me hollow. "I still don't understand why you didn't tell me."

We make our way into my yard and sit on the garden bench.

"Habit, I guess. There were a few girls who were more interested in what I could buy them than me, so I stopped talking about my parents to girls. I know it was stupid, but I was a bit thrown you lived on the same street as my parents. I stuck to my game plan."

We sit in silence for a while, but I take a chance and stare into his eyes. "You have a game plan?"

The relief seems to wash over him as he goes from rigid to loose all at once. "Of course."

"And how is your game plan working so far?"

"Perfectly."

He leans in, and this time, I let him kiss me. I reach up and push my fingers through his hair, eager for more. All my negative thoughts wash away as I lose myself in Ryder. He trails his tongue over my lips, sending butterflies dancing in my stomach. From above comes the sound of a clearing throat. "Ahem."

Dad glowers over us. "Your mother is looking for you. She wants to start."

We jump apart, holding our laughter until Dad retreats inside.

"Whoops." Ryder gulps. "Busted, again."

"He'll get over it. But Mum mightn't if we don't get in there."

We race upstairs together, jostling to get through the door at the same time, and then spill into the lounge. Mum and Dad sit in their usual places while Ryder and I take the floor. I nestle between his legs and rest my head against his chest. Dad insists on putting his Santa hat on and starts handing out the presents.

I tear at the wrapping paper on Ryder's present. A Saint Christopher's key glimmers on top of a book of Shakespeare quotes. I pick up the note: *To make sure you always get safely home.*

I told Mum not to go all out because I didn't want to embarrass Ryder with the whole social gap thing, but I'm glad she ignored me. He ends up having more presents than me.

At lunch, Dad tells a series of stories about his childhood as well as some embarrassing episodes from my youth. Ryder laughs when he should and shoots me sympathetic glances. He has no idea he'll get them from me after he hears that story for the tenth time.

Once we're all so full to exploding, I motion to

Ryder to help with the dishes. I clear the table, he rinses, and we both stack the dishwasher. It's going to be two loads. Occasionally, our hands touch and each time bursts of happiness explode in my chest.

The deck is the best place to be on a hot summer's day. Dad tests the new pool lounger he got from Mum while Ryder gets ready for a swim. *Oh yeah, the boy's got just the right amount of definition in his chest, abs, and biceps.* Stripped down to his shorts, Ryder eases into the water.

I shed my clothes and join him. It's hard to find swimwear that hides my scar, but with Ryder's reaction I don't care about it and happily show off in my bikini. We play around a bit, but Dad's ever-watchful gaze spoils any opportunity for more. I let Ryder scoop me into his arms. My fingers trail over his tattoos.

"What do these mean?" I trace my fingers over a series of symbols. *Celtic or Gaelic?* The lettering reminds me of the elfish writing in *The Lord of the Rings*. They weave around his right bicep and chest in delicate scrolls and patterns. His left arm has one tattoo where his arm meets his shoulder that I hadn't seen before. It appears like the outline of a butterfly, embellished with a multiple layer frame of finely twisted metal. I've seen similar pendants in new age shops but never with this much detail.

Ryder raises an eyebrow. "To be honest, I do not know. I sketched them in art at high school and kept them aside. I took them in when I decided to get a tattoo and this was the result." His gaze moves toward his parents' house. "Mum and Dad will be back from their Christmas lunch soon. Did you want to come down and meet them?"

"I'd love to." My hands clap together.

Ryder stares at me, but it's more than that—he seems to see into me. "You are the most beautiful person I have ever met. Not just seen, but met." Dad or no Dad, he kisses me and brings me closer to him. It's electrifying. In the end, I put my hands on his shoulders and push us apart, half expecting Dad to dive into the pool and wallop Ryder.

Out of the corner of my eye, I see Mum herding Dad inside the house. That leaves Smelly Belly as our sole audience.

Ryder continues staring at me, his eyes smoldering with desire, but I want to make sure they're fully inside before we pick up where we left off. "So what are we going to do for New Year's?"

"That depends on what you want to do?" He reaches forward and trails a fingertip along my jaw.

"I'm not sure, but I know what I want right now." There's been enough time since my family's exit. I go in for more kisses.

When our lips part, Ryder says, "Well, I know what I want right now too." He sounds very serious.

"What's that?"

"To watch you fly."

I have barely enough time to scrunch my nose in confusion before being swept up and flung across the pool. I hit the surface hard and submerge. I come up coughing, pain searing my chest. I wince and clutch at my scar.

"Mishca, I am so sorry. I did not think," says Ryder filled with horror.

My voice fails me. Lungs, throat, and nose all burn down to my insides. I inhale, willing my heart to stop controlling me. Water churns around me as Ryder does this weird run-swim to me. He puts a hand on me. I take another breath and my pulse eases.

"It's okay," I reply and splash water in Ryder's face. "But you deserve that." We exchange water blows, inching closer to each other. I leap up and land with my hands on his head to push him under.

As he resurfaces, he locks his hands around my wrists, preventing further splashage. We goggle at each other, grinning like idiots. Ryder kisses me again, more deeply than before, taking advantage of our solitude. He laces his fingers through mine. I lose track of time as we stay locked together. When we come up for air, I can't help giggling.

"What?" He cocks a brow.

I point down. "You have grandpa hands."

He glances at his shriveled fingers. Then, grabs my hand and kisses my matching wrinkled fingers.

"Definitely a sign we are done."

He climbs out with his shorts clinging to him and offers me a hand. He brings me up into a big wet bear hug. I rest my head on his chest, listening to his heartbeat, and suddenly, I understand why so many of my friends disappear off the radar when a guy comes into their lives.

Is this love? Hopefully.

I lie on a pool chair, letting the sun dry my skin. Ryder focuses on nothing but me. At least he appears to have it as bad as I do. It doesn't take long for the droplets of water to evaporate so we get changed—separately, of course. Mum might be okay with some open affection, but she has her limits on what shenanigans will go on in the house. I may be eighteen but as Dad likes to say, "their house, their rules."

I decide a nice sundress is the way to go instead of the habitual denim mini and t-shirt combo I've been wearing since my operation. It's so much easier to get high-necked t-shirts than dresses; however, this one has a higher lace bodice that obscures my scar. Its soft beige material with pink and yellow flowers sets off my skin well. I slip on my taupe flat sandals and wait for Ryder to come out from the bathroom. He appears, nearly jumping out of his skin with excitement.

"Ready?" he says, extending his hand. I nod.

We travel down the street and stop at the

Spanish villa-style home Ryder came out of earlier. The moisture builds on my hands when we reach the stairs. He gives me a squeeze, and then hits the buzzer. An enquiring voice comes through the telecom. Ryder hits the buzzer again. "Just me."

The clicking of heels echoes from behind the front door. Ryder's mother appears with a smile that gets wider when she sees me, though I can also read a small hint of confusion.

"Ryder, honey, we weren't expecting to see you again so soon and especially not with a friend." She says the word *friend* rather pointedly with a slight British accent. He gives her a kiss on the cheek.

"Mum, this is my girlfriend, Mish—"

His mother rushes in a response before Ryder can finish. "Yes. You're Tom and Alicia's girl. I see your mother at the club. It's so wonderful to meet you. How are you feeling?" Her gaze lingers on the fabric covering my chest.

"It's lovely to meet you too, and I'm fine, thank you." I say the words but squirm inside. I'm damaged. I'll be deemed unsuitable, not good enough to be with her son.

"Good to see you have blessed us with your presence again." A hint of sarcasm as Ryder's dad appears. "Oh, and you've brought company."

"Hello, Mr. Madson. Great to meet you."

He extends his hand and grips mine firmly. "No need for formalities. Call me George."

"Yes, and call me Martha," pipes in Ryder's mum.

"Well, come on in you two. No point standing out there."

No one would put it together that Ryder's adopted. His dad has salt and pepper in what remains of his hair and a moustache with paler skin. His mother has blue eyes that could easily be interpreted as a maternal link. None of their facial features scream *relative*, but they don't discount it either.

We follow them onto the patio where they're having afternoon drinks. I turn down a brandy as does Ryder.

"So how does your father think his boys will do this year?"

"Good. They bought some new players and—"

"Hmm, that's nice. How about that captain? He had an operation on his shoulder at the end of the season, if I'm not mistaken. Will he be able to return for round one?"

Ryder pinches the bridge of his nose. "Father, please."

"I'm not sure," I say. "I don't keep track of the team that closely."

"Ah." He sounds disappointed. "Well, be back in a bit."

I score a silent wince of apology from Ryder, though I'm not sure what I've missed. Sure his father might be pushy on rugby, but that's no big deal. Mrs. Madson holds out a plate of food. I grab a dried fig and nibble.

"Will you two be at the same university next year?" Mrs. Madson asks.

"I haven't received my offers yet. They'll come through in the New Year."

"Oh." She puts the platter down and turns to Ryder. "Have you switched over to engineering as we suggested?"

"No," he replies through his teeth. "Still studying environmental law."

Mr. Madson returns, paper in hand and folded to the races pages. Ryder makes a move to go. I can see the disappointment etched on his mother's face.

"What about the Fitness Factory?" says Mrs. Madson.

"Still working there," Ryder replies. "Do I smell the Chanel No. 5 I got you?"

"Yes, dear. although I don't know how you can afford it on your income." She pauses. "If you came home you would be so much closer to Mishca. You could see more of her."

My mouth falls open, almost losing the nibble of fig.

"Mother, really."

Mr. Madson grunts and continues reading.

"Mishca, do you ever go on shoots with your mum?" Mrs. Madson takes a sip from her glass, and then rests it on the table.

"Sometimes," I reply.

"Do you plan on following in her footsteps?"

"No. I'm going to focus on university." I'm not sure if her question is serious or not as I'm far too short to model fashion. Shorter girls can do swimsuit modeling, but they're usually more ample breasted than I am...and don't have an ugly scar.

"What do you want to study?" She sounds genuine. I glance over at Ryder. He seems to be enjoying the conversation. Mr. Madson puts the paper down and heads off to the kitchen.

"I'd love QUT's drama program, but it's tough to get into." Mum took me to an audition before my operation. My bravest jump into drama thus far. The panel gave me no idea how it went.

"So you've still got the show biz bug, just a different area."

"You could say that." I rub a hand through my hair. It's not true. I'm a fraud. I've never acted before, unless you count drama class. Dad drummed it into me that there are a lot of out-of-work actors, so I might have to consider other occupations in the area—if I get in. I don't say any of that though and try not to let it show on my face. "I might do law."

"Environmental law?" asks Ryder, a hopeful wisp in his voice.

I shrug. "I'm not sure. Dad wants me to study it.

I haven't researched it too much."

Mr. Madson returns with an imported beer in hand and joins the conversation. We stay for about an hour. The awkwardness slips away, and by the time we leave, I'm glad we came.

We walk down the path toward my house hand-in-hand. Ryder stops at his car, leans against it, and draws me to him. *Boom-boom, boom-boom.* It's so comforting, the sound of his heart. We stay locked together for what feels like an eternity before he kisses me on the top of the head.

"Better go inside before I get another scolding from your dad." He's trying to make a joke, but there's a hint of fear in his voice.

I throw back my head and laugh. "You're risking my mum stuffing you full of leftovers from lunch once we're in there."

"That is a risk I am willing to take."

CHAPTER 12

"MISHCA." THE SOUND *makes me shudder before the blackness consumes me.* "Mishca." *I hear the haunting voice calling my name but see nothing through the mist.* "Mishca. Come to me."

I ignore the hidden source and search around me for a clue to my whereabouts.

"Mum! Dad!" *I shout for my parents. After no reply, I try again, fear rising in my chest.* "Mum! Dad!"

"They do not want you anymore." *The voice comes from all around me.* "You are not good enough. You have failed them as a daughter. You will always fail them. Come to me. This is where you are meant to be."

I curl into a ball and cover my ears. No, it's not true. They love me. I'm theirs. I've always been theirs. My thoughts try to run wild with fear, but I will them to focus on my parents and their love.

"Do not fight me, Mishca. You are mine." *Harsh laughter fills my head.*

"No! I am his!"

Sucking in air, I release my clenched fists.

"Hey, are you okay?" Ryder whispers in my ear, his body pressed against mine as we lay side-by-side. Mum and Dad caved in and let him stay over, though he's supposed to be in the guest room downstairs.

"It's nothing," I fib, not able to meet his gaze.

"That did not sound like nothing. You were thrashing about like crazy."

"It was a nightmare. I get them sometimes. It's another delightful side effect of my medication."

I press my lips together to make sure nothing else slips out. My first serious boyfriend won't last very long if he discovers the rest of my weirdness.

Ryder traces the line of my scar with a fingertip. "Have you told your doctor about them? Or your hallucinations?"

"No, but it's not a big deal. Everyone reacts to the recovery process differently. There are worse side effects to have." I entwine our fingers and change the subject. "So what are we up to today?"

He nods. "I was contemplating going to a meeting."

"They hold them on the holidays?"

"Sometimes that is the hardest time when you are missing a loved one, even if that loved one is someone unknown to you." Ryder starts kissing my neck. The fluttery touches make me shiver and shudder.

"But you're not alone. You have me." I roll over to face him.

"I know. But Sherry said she may have some news. I am itching to find out."

I playfully slap his arm. "Why didn't you tell me?"

"Ouch." He rubs his arm.

"Sorry." I frown.

"There was no point in getting both our hopes up."

My fingers run through his hair as I kiss him. His hands find my hips, and he clasps me to him. Our kiss deepens. Ryder's hand moves upward over my flimsy pajama top. My mind flashes back to when he snuck in my room early this morning. We'd kissed for so long my lips went numb, but I thought I heard Dad, so I put on the brakes. I pause, and then put my lips to his again.

"Breakfast is ready," Mum says from the doorway, making us jump apart. "And Dad will be out of bed soon so I suggest, Ryder, you're out of Mishca's room in less than two minutes."

I glimpse a wide-eyed Ryder and giggle. Then, he bolts for the door, grinning.

"Shower's free, honey." Dad sticks his head in my room. Not too subtle; normally, I find out if it's free by him wandering past.

"Thanks, Dad." I give him my best innocent face adding, "Why don't you check to see if Ryder's up and tell him he can have a shower after me?"

Even though it's still the morning, my skin prickles and my pajamas stick to me. I step in the shower. My body embraces the water as it cascades over me. I don't hang around in there today, not wanting to leave Ryder alone with my dad for too long.

I yank open the door, and there's Ryder, waiting for his turn.

"You're still a bit dirty. Better get back in." His gorgeous grin teases me.

"You wish," I retort.

"Yes, I do."

I give him a peck on the cheek as I scoot past. Ryder reaches for me, but I duck past his hands and head downstairs for breakfast.

The meeting doesn't feel like the best idea for today. When he meets me at the table, he must sense my apprehension. "It will be fine." His hand cups my chin, lifting my face to his. "There could be news. I need to go."

"Okay," I whisper.

* * * *

Ryder and I walk into the meeting hand-in-hand, which gets a smirk out of Sherry. We have our pick of chairs today, so we sit close to the refreshments. I recognize some people from the last time. Trista skips through the door as the meeting starts, beaming. She sits beside me and gives my leg a squeeze before waving madly at Ryder.

Sherry stands up to begin. "Well, we have no new people today, so we might skip the introductions and go to open discussion." Ryder stares at Sherry. "Paul, would you like to start?" Sherry indicates the middle-aged man to her left.

Paul clears his throat. "Christmas was hard. I went to see my mother." He begins to choke up. "M-my half-brother H-Herbert wouldn't l-let me in her house. He doesn't b-believe I'm hers."

Sherry pats his hand. "Does anyone have something to share for Paul?"

A young woman opposite me speaks up and talks about her denial when discovering her younger aunt was actually her mum. The only advice is to give Paul's half-brother time. Sherry motions to the next person to speak.

"I gave up my son for adoption straight away after he was born. He's all grown up now with a family of his own. I met my son's family for the first time before Christmas." The woman has hard lifelines scattered across her face. "His two girls are so excited to have a third grandmother. I brought their Christmas presents with me, but they asked me to come over on Christmas Day." Her wrinkled face lights up and her eyes dance even more.

"I have nothing new to add," says the young woman opposite me. "Everything has been pretty good between us all for a while now." A peek at the faces around the room and it's obvious I'm not the only one who envies her.

When it skips around to Ryder's turn, he says, "I have nothing new," his gaze doesn't leave Sherry's face, "yet."

Heads swivel in my direction at my turn. "I have nothing new." My shoulders slump. *And I never will.*

Trista begins gabbling some nonsense about her discovery that she's the only one of her siblings who doesn't have a baby scan, but my mind wanders lost in thoughts of the family I'll never be able to find.

The meeting ends not long after Trista's turn due to the poor turnout and since people have places to be. Ryder loiters, catching Sherry's eye again. I can't read her face at all.

She doesn't even wait for Ryder to ask. "I'm afraid it was a false alarm, Ryder. The people we found were another set of parents who had you in their care temporarily. But we're getting close. Hang in there."

Ryder's chin tilts down, lips set in a straight line. His shoulders rise and fall with the sigh that escapes. "Okay."

We head to the parking lot and get into Ryder's car without a word. The silence stays settled over us until we pull up at my place.

Out of nowhere, Ryder gives the steering wheel

a thump. "It was so close. I was sure they had found them this time!" He faces me, his gloomy expression matching mine. "Mishca, I am sorry. Every step is still a step closer to finding them."

I say nothing, my jaw clenched tight. I resist the urge to punch something in case I do some major damage. "Mishca, what is wrong?"

"I'm never going to find my birth parents."

"Oh, Mishca." Ryder embraces me. "I did not even think about that. I was caught up in me."

"I don't want to go there again."

Ryder strokes my hair. "You do not have to, babe."

CHAPTER 13

MY FINGER HOVERS above the touch pad on my laptop. My future sits one click away.

"Come on, Mishca," says Mum, almost whining like it's a Christmas present that's arrived two weeks late and needs opening.

I breathe out and press down to open my offer page. Something twists inside me.

"Bachelor of Arts?" Dad says. "I thought you were going to study law."

I bite my lip. Missing out on being a lawyer doesn't bum me out. But not getting into the drama course kills me. I'd thrown arts in to fill up some slots, as a backup I never thought I'd need. "Arts was like my fifth preference. I don't understand either."

"It's okay," says Mum, trying her best to sound reassuring. "You can always accept arts and swap over later. Or maybe you'll get into law or drama on the second round of offers."

I push the swelling anger down. "It's fine." I stand up, not game to touch the laptop in case the Hyde-side of me comes out and smashes it. "I'm going to go over to Ryder's for a bit."

"Sure thing, honey."

"You can't spend all summer there, though." Dad wags a finger at me. "You're not going to have this much free time at university."

I resist the urge to roll my eyes. I've barely seen Ryder these holidays. He's taken up a second job so he's got enough money for uni. I leave without so much as a goodbye. Once in Betsy, I get some relief. My knuckles grip the steering wheel with measured control the whole thirty-minute drive. My wheels crunch against the gravel when I pull onto his road and head toward the shed, hoping he'll be home. I can't seem to get my nerves down enough to even remember what shifts he's working this week.

"At least Ryder and I will be together at uni," I whisper, trying to stem the wave of bitterness.

I march to the door, eager to have Ryder's arms around me, for him to tell me it'll all be okay. Instead, I'm greeted by a locked back door. *Maybe it's jammed.* I yank harder. A loud *crack* accompanies wood splinters shooting past me. The door falls away from its hinges.

Crap!

"Have you been sneaking over here to pump

our weights? Cause that was pretty bad arse."

I whip around. Finlay stares at me with an eyebrow raised. He strides over and grabs the door from me, almost as effortlessly as it came off the frame.

"I-I don't know what happened," I manage to reply.

Finlay gives me a peculiar look, like I'm something that crawled out of the Black Lagoon, and sets about repairing the door.

I can't ignore this creepiness for too much longer. Maybe I should tell Dr. Thompson my new heart has come with a side of super strength, hearing, and speed. Something is up, big time, but I've already lived too many years of my life as the outcast with the weak heart. I don't want to be in a new freak category.

What if they put me in a lab? Or worse, a straightjacket?

"Here, come hold this." Finlay gestures to the door.

I inch over and follow his instructions.

"What was that?" he asks, keeping his eyes on his work.

"I can't explain it because I don't know." I bite my lip.

"Does Ryder know?"

I shake my head as he peers over his shoulder at me.

"You're not going to tell Ryder, are you?" he says, before the sound of his electric drill stops any opportunity for an immediate response.

"I ... ah." Fear ripples through me at the thought of Ryder rejecting me.

"Don't worry. I won't tell him yet." He stands up and tests the door. It swings easily. He reaches out and grabs my shoulder, his fingers biting in. I suppress a wince. "But if I think for one moment that you are a threat to him, I will end you."

Hostile behavior detected. I recoil, both at Finlay's words and the clinical voice in my head, but his hand stays firm. I resist the urge to grab him and throw him across the backyard.

I glare at him. "I would never hurt Ryder."

The sound of tires on gravel makes Finlay drop his hand and step away.

Ryder waves as he drives past to park his car beside mine. I flash him my best fake smile ever and keep it plastered on my face, despite the residual throbbing of Finlay's touch. *How has he managed to hurt me like that?* My pain threshold has been crazy off the charts, along with everything else.

Finlay plops on the hammock and swings nonchalantly as Ryder saunters over.

"Hey, beautiful."

I tilt my head back for a kiss. For a moment, I forget we have an audience, but then I pull away.

"What is wrong?"

I resist the urge to peek at Finlay to see the expression on his face. "Nothing."

"Wait, your uni offers come in today, right?"

My face screws up like someone shoved sulfur under my nose. "Ugh, yes. And I didn't get into any of my top choices."

"That's too bad," says Finlay from the hammock.

I glare at him, wishing the ability to shoot lightning bolts from my eyes was amongst my freaky powers. Ryder frowns at his friend, and then returns his attention to me.

"Are you okay?"

The concern in his voice melts away the tension constricting my body and emotions.

"I'll be fine. At least we'll be at uni together. And it'll give me time to figure what I want to do."

Jelly Roll shuffles over with a snort and bares his belly for rubs beside me. At least he's not setting off my danger alerts. Looking at the size of his stomach, he doesn't event pose a threat to the neighborhood cats.

"What are we going to do for your birthday?"

I shrug. Two weeks isn't too far away in reality, but I haven't planned anything. Nineteen is such a nothing birthday. Last year officially as a teenager, a bit of an anticlimax. "Probably a family dinner if you want to come over."

Ryder still doesn't feel one hundred percent

comfortable around Dad. Maybe Mum's over the top chocolate cake will fill them both with enough sugar that they'll fall into a sweet stupor and forget they saw me in my bra at the same time.

"Sounds perfect."

Ryder walks towards the house with Finlay in tow, chatting about some upcoming sporting event that isn't rugby league so I have no idea what it is.

"I'll be in soon," I call and find myself trudging over to the fence. I start pacing around the perimeter. *I'm doing a perimeter sweep? Mishca, get it together.*

Threat detected. A tingling that has become far too familiar ripples through my body. I refuse to give into this and follow Ryder inside, abandoning my security checks.

CHAPTER 14

FINLAY'S KEPT HIS promise. I still haven't told Ryder about the strange side effects...or Dr. Thompson. The past month has been torture. Ryder's needed to build up some savings for the start of uni so he took on full-time hours at the sports store and we've barely seen each other. And when we do Finlay is right there, hounding me like he thinks I'm going turn into some praying mantis and devour his best friend. In fact, he's given Ryder and I almost zero alone time. Major third-wheel. I've been very careful not to break anything else, but Finlay still watches me.

It's like there's two of me battling inside: one that's completely freaked out by what's going on, and one that says everything will be okay and not to overreact. Instead of doing anything, I've let these little subconscious versions of me battle it out in my head. But now school's started and with it my determination to put it all behind me.

I walk alone through the maze of older and more modern-styled university buildings, excited about starting the next chapter of my life. Map clutched in hand, I check the names of buildings against my guide, wishing Ryder was here with me. His first class started before I even arrived on campus and it'll be hours before we're both free.

As I finally figure out the direction to my first lecture, *Introduction to Classic and Modern Literature*, a voice calls, "Mishca. Wait up." Nerissa scrambles toward me, clutching a bundle of books to her chest. "Do you mind if we go together?" She motions to my textbook. The huge title makes my destination clear.

"Sure," I respond, surprised but happy to have the company of a familiar face. "Not a prob."

Nerissa flicks her long blond hair over her shoulder, unaware of the many guys and girls watching her—some of them drooling. We walk a few steps in silence before I bite. "So where is the rest of the group?"

Nerissa's face screws up. "Sorry?"

"Um nothing, sorry. Where are Dorian, Nixie, and the others?" I reply, referring to her high school clique.

"Oh, well, I'm not studying the same course as them." Nerissa chews on her bottom lip like I've touched on a sore spot.

"Ah, so what are they studying?" My curiosity hits its peak.

"Marine biology."

"What? All five of them?"

Nerissa nods in response. "Yep, I'm the black sheep. And my parents totally freaked when they found I'd swapped my major this year."

"I understand. Dad wanted me to study law, I wanted to study acting, and I ended up in arts. But it's not as bad as I thought since I can still major in drama. It's studying the plays at least. My other classes aren't bad."

"What else are you going to study?" she asks as we stride in sync.

"So far drama, literature, and film and television studies. I'm taking some peace and conflict subjects for fun too. What about you?"

"Literature, of course, anthropology, and archaeology. I love old stuff."

We both giggle, letting free some nervous energy.

"Have you checked what we'll be reading?" I wave the large textbook.

"Mainly the contents page. I'm looking forward to the Brontë sisters." She grimaces as she tries to hold up the textbook one-handed and readjusts her grip.

"Hmm." I shift my other hand down and grasp my books with both hands to mimic Nerissa's strain. "I only got into *Wuthering Heights* and *Jane Eyre*."

"Let me guess — Jane Austen?"

I pull a face. "Of course."

"Isn't that a bit, um, conventional? I mean, it kinda goes without saying." Nerissa returns the face.

"I know, but the innocence of *Emma*, the trials of *Sense and Sensibility*, and the magic of *Pride and Prejudice*."

"Have you read *Pride and Prejudice and Zombies*?" Nerissa asks, a cautious edge of excitement creeping into her voice.

"Not yet, but I want to. And the Mr Darcy vampire one too." I pause to check the map. "I think this is us."

I hesitate at the threshold of the auditorium, and then purposefully, take my first step in. I survey the room but don't recognize any other face there. Nerissa makes me feel safe amongst the sea of more than a hundred students. The large domed room has row after row of seats filled. We take two open spots at the front.

Some students have small desks in front of them that are about the size of an airplane tray table. I carefully maneuver my moveable desk hanging beside my chair. I don't want to scare off Nerissa by breaking the thing. When I get it moving in the right direction, it swivels in front of Nerissa instead of me.

"Thanks," she laughs as I get mine into position.

"How's work going?" I ask, wishing I had a part-time job, especially in a clothes shop. But an after school job was never an option before.

Nerissa scrunches up her nose. "I'm not there anymore. They wanted me to work more hours, but I couldn't with uni. I've got an interview at Super Sundaes next week. It should be an easy job; although, it might be very bad for my waist."

A short young man with cropped blond hair and pale skin enters the auditorium and takes position behind the podium. A hush settles over the students. I glance at Nerissa. Professor Read, our noted lecturer, appears much younger than I expected. He can't be more than twenty-five and has a hot in a scruffy skateboarder vibe. He clears his throat and steps up to the microphone.

"Good morning to you all. Wonderful to see another year of fervent students ready to absorb all there is to know about the great English classics. My name is Paul Schultz, but most people call me Sarge." He smiles at the crowd. "If you can work that out, why then, you are a pop culture buff and earn yourself first choice of presentation topic in the tutorial, but not the option to go last. Most of you were probably expecting the infamous Professor Colin Read, but unfortunately, he's unwell and will be joining us as soon as he's better. Now, onto what you can look forward to in this class."

Sarge drones on about the course outline, assessments, and textbooks we need to purchase. Finally, he pauses to take a breath and ask if we have any questions. Timidly, I raise my hand.

Cocking his eyebrows in surprise, Sarge responds, "Yes, go ahead eager beaver." That scores a flurry of smirks and giggles from the group. Sarge blushes at his error.

"Hogan's Heroes?" I say. Dad loves the show and has forced me to sit through endless reruns, so I am well acquainted with the lovable and tubby Sergeant Schultz.

"Very good..."

I try to get my mouth to work as he waits for my name. "Mishca. Mishca Richardson."

"Very good, Mishca. Now class, no tutorials for week one, but I have signup sheets here that you will need to put your name on before leaving." He ceremoniously places them in front of me, so Nerissa and I have first dibs on tutorial times. We can't help grinning. Teacher's pet rules don't seem to apply the same way at uni as they did at school, and I'm happy to be off on the right foot.

We both scribble our names into the same tutorial group and settle in to listen to the rest of the lecture. It's not as interesting as I'd hoped, but mainly because it's the introduction, unit outline, and assessments details with a small bit touching on the topic, the Brontë sisters.

"Do you have a class now?" asks Nerissa as we exit the lecture hall.

I shake my head. "No, I've got a few free hours."

"Me too. You want to hang out?"

"Sure."

We find a bench seat overlooking a large grassy quad. Students sit around, some on the lawn and others on seats.

"What did you think of the lecture?" A voice comes to me from a girl across the quad as she walks with another student toward administration, some hundred meters away.

"It was okay. At least Sarge was cute. I won't complain if we have him instead of Professor Read."

I close my eyes and inhale deeply, focusing on blocking them. For an hour, I was normal. No thoughts about stupid powers. No reminders I'm an aberration. It was nice while it lasted. But I can make it last, if I just pretend.

CHAPTER 15

ONE DAY AFTER CLASS, Nerissa spots a spare shady patch of grass near the fountain so we head over to stake our claim. Uni has rocked so far. Classes have been fun. Things have been great with Ryder. I've learned to control myself a lot more so I break fewer things, and I haven't overheard a conversation unintentionally in a while. Plus, Nerissa and I have been having a blast together.

Nerissa never socialized much outside of her clique when we were at school. But our rapport was instantaneous, which is why I'm hesitant to broach what's on my mind.

"So you remember when I asked why you weren't with the others?" I suck in a breath.

"Yes."

"Well, that is, you, your brother, and your group…" I struggle to find the right words. "It's just you were all so exclusive with each other back then.

But you never talk to me about them now, and I've never met them."

Suddenly, the grass becomes very interesting to Nerissa, and she starts pulling bits out blade by blade. She sighs and makes eye-contact with me. "I'm not meant to talk about it. Not like it's a big secret or anything either. Well, it is, sort of. But I can trust you, right?"

Her eyes plead with me. I nod.

"When all of our parents discovered they were pregnant they decided to come to Australia to start over. I'm not even sure where they came from. It's a taboo topic. They wanted to make sure we were born here. All I know is it was a small European country, and there was a lot of repression, especially against people with our parents'...ah, heritage."

Nerissa must sense my skepticism as she blurts out, "We were raised differently than most kids our age. All of our parents were—and still are—very strict. They've all said when we're old enough, they'll tell us everything. We know some stuff about our heritage, but we're all in the dark on why our parents had to leave."

"Okaaay." I drawl, trying to take it all in. "But why no mixing with anyone else?"

"Protection strategy. When they left they were on the run, so staying together helped keep them safe. And well, there is—" Nerissa stops short and groans, burying her head in her hands. "You're not going to understand."

"Try me." I do my best to sound as reassuring as I can.

"Okay, well, we are all kinda betrothed."

"Get out!" I can't help myself. "As in polygamy, but multiple husbands *and* wives?"

"Mishca! No, not like that! Ew! No! I'm betrothed to Dylan, Dorian is betrothed to Nerine, and Nixie is betrothed to Douglas. It's been arranged since we were born. Our parents thought it would protect our bloodlines."

"But wait, you went out with Douglas last year."

Crimson hives rise up Nerissa's neck. "Our lame attempt at rebellion."

I sit for a minute, soaking it in. "Okay, so it's not much different than many immigrants who want their kids to marry within their culture."

She greets my comment with silence. My brows pinch together at my tactlessness. Curiosity killed the cat, and I only hope it won't kill our friendship.

"You don't think I'm a freak, do you?" asks Nerissa.

I have to stop from recoiling in shame. "No, of course not. Hey, if anyone's a freak around here, it's the chick with the scarred chest and constant nightmares!"

The words slip free before I can stop them. The operation wasn't a secret, but the nightmares — my parents and Ryder alone are privy to that info. And only Ryder knows about my hallucinations. Nerissa's forehead creases. The side of her mouth twitches as though she wants to say something but can't work out what.

As if on cue, Ryder strolls across the grass and drops beside me. Nerissa glances at me but says nothing about my comment. Ryder slings his arm around my shoulders and kisses me on the cheek. "Hey, you."

"Hey, you back." I nuzzle him, drinking in his aftershave. Uni is seriously cutting into our time together, but I shouldn't complain. For the first time in a long time, I'm happy — almost completely content. If I could take away those pesky dreams, odd accidents, and the guilt I feel for putting Dad and Mum through so much shit this summer, things would be almost perfect.

I have Ryder and it's bordering on the L-word. I've got a new close female friend — oh, and I love uni. Maybe this could be the best year ever after all.

* * * *

"Ryder, Ryder, where are you?" Fog swirls through the darkness. "Nerissa? Anybody?" Around me there is nothing but mist and shadows. I stumble forward. "Please don't leave me. I'm sorry." My hands reach into the black, groping for anything. But there is nothing.

"Forget Ryder. He will leave you, abandon you. Just like your mother." The voice snakes through my mind,

and my head starts to ache.

Confusion clouds my brain. Mum has never left me. I clutch handfuls of hair as I curl into a ball, praying the voice will go away. The dreams are worse when he's in them.

"Not her. Not the one pretending to be your mother. Your real mother." I recoil at his invasion of my inner thoughts. "Your prayers won't save you. Give in now and come to me."

"No!" I jump and run away from the voice, stumbling as I go. Then, the man with the long brown hair materializes before me.

"Run if you like, Mishca, I will always be able to catch you," he sniggers. "Always."

I awake with a start and glance at the clock, glad to have shaken off the bad dream. *Four in the morning!* Still in a haze, I fumble around on my bedside table, groping for my nightlight. I hate going straight to sleep after a dream like that in case another one follows. I swing my legs out of bed and toddle over to my desk to grab my peace and conflict studies books.

I've been neglecting them in favor of my drama and literature subjects; studying peace isn't as enticing as I thought it would be. *Mental note to self: check if I can drop it now without penalty.*

Smelly Belly ambles into my room and attacks the sheets hanging from my bed. She claws up the side, ripping at the material, until she hauls herself beside me, purring like crazy.

I abandon my uni books and snuggle with my cat as the gentle nuzzles elicit more pats. It only takes a few minutes for the nagging head butts to stop, and then sleep overtakes us both.

The dreams stay away, and when I wake for the second time, I'm more refreshed. Mum pops her head around the corner and tries her hardest to appear stern about my sleep-in instead of amused by the cat curled up on my pillow. The twitching at the corners of her mouth means she isn't pulling it off well. "You ready for breakfast?"

"Sure, what's on offer? Bacon?" I can't help but tease.

"No, fruit and cereal." Boy, she has no sense of humor sometimes.

My tousled hair can't be ignored, so I jump in the shower before heading down. I love the lack of dress code for uni after so many years of plaid school uniforms, and it's a great excuse for shopping expeditions. I'm still not ready to wear clothes that reveal my scar, which does restrict my wardrobe a bit.

I head downstairs to the kitchen where Mum already has everything waiting. The house is quieter than normal with the new season games underway for Dad. He's in Sydney for an upcoming match. I've swallowed my first mouthful when May-Lee enters the dining room followed by Ryder.

"Hey, you're early!" I can't stop myself from

running over to plant a kiss on his lips. I jump up and wrap my legs around him, which results in us both falling in a heap on the ground. Not the romantic scene I envisioned in my head.

Ryder groans.

"Are you okay?"

"A bit winded. Have you been doing tackling drills with your dad?"

"Just excited to see you." I smile.

"I need to find another reference book for an assignment so I thought I would head in earlier before class. You want to come with me now?" He glances expectantly at Mum, but she sits still, her mouth twitching as though she's suppressing a smirk.

"Sure. Let me get my bag."

I race upstairs. Every moment with Ryder excites me. Even though we've been taking things nice and slow, I think Ryder's still a tad scared of Dad after the scar incident. Secretly, I've been wishing my first serious boyfriend would be my last. It would be a story as romantic as any of Austen's—to have a one and only love. I'm downstairs fast and already planning how to use the extra time to see if I can drop history. I give Mum a peck on the cheek, and then grab Ryder's hand, aiming to maximize our time together.

"What about breakfast? And your pills."

I respond by darting to the bench, grabbing an

apple and the medication before disappearing out the door, Ryder in tow.

* * * *

"Hmm, I love kissing you," I murmur. Understatement of the year. If I could I would do virtually nothing else.

Ryder gazes at me, tracing my jaw line with his finger. "I love more than just kissing you." Not waiting for a response, he brushes his mouth gently against mine before trailing the tip of his tongue over my lips. We've found a secluded grassy cove nestled amongst trees behind the library.

Unexpectedly, Ryder wrenches away and stares at the book he'd grabbed for his class. "I need to tell you something."

I straighten up. "Sure, is anything wrong?"

"No. Well, I have some news."

"Don't keep me in suspense then." I bounce on the balls of my feet, trying not to rush him.

"I think I may have found my mother."

I stop cold, still as a marble statue. I haven't been going to the support meetings and we don't talk about our biological family search much lately. While I still have a burning desire to discover my roots that flame is a match head compared to the inferno I feel for Ryder. I'd almost forgotten he's still actively looking.

"Oh." Ryder's face falls at my pitiful response.

"No, I mean that's good. So how did you find her?"

"I will tell you more tonight, I promise."

"Sure thing." I am happy for him, despite the painful reminder of my situation.

He's quiet, picking at blades of grass and deep in thought.

"Mishca, do you ever feel different? Like you don't fit in or belong?"

I flinch. *Am I that transparent? Does he know about my abnormalities?*

"Um, never mind," mumbles Ryder. "I have got to fly or I will not get to class on time. I will see you this afternoon. Meet me out front," Ryder says, hopping up to leave.

I watch him walk off into the distance from the front of the library. Inside I'm empty and hollow. *Why did I freeze up? Whatever it was obviously meant a lot to him.* A tap on my shoulder brings me back to earth, and I turn to see Nerissa's beaming face.

We enter the room buzzed for class. Sarge is in the last row instead of at the front. He gives me a stiff nod and mock salute. I grin in return as Nerissa and I take our seats. We hunch together so the bustle of students around us are not privy to our debate.

"Have you two, you know?" I shake my head at her question. "Don't you believe in trying before you buy?"

"Nerissa!" I squeal as quietly as I can. "Didn't

you notice the guys at school didn't want to date an invalid?" I tap my chest.

"Not really," Nerissa says. "Douglas thought you were hot. I caught him trying to perv a peek up your skirt when you went up the stairs once." She shoots me an evil grin.

Suddenly, a tingling presence pulls at my very soul. The world goes into slow motion and all noise ceases to exist.

My gaze drags up to the figure that has passed through the door. *Boom-ba-boom.* He is...he is... My mouth goes dry. Beads of sweat threaten to form. *Boom-ba-ba-boom.* I take a deep breath and calm myself, steadying my heart. But it won't be still. There's nothing in the room now but him and me. The man before me, taking his place behind the lectern, is a part of me. He is *the one*.

CHAPTER 16

MY HEART CONTINUES to pound in my chest. *Who is this man, and why am I so attracted to him?*

It's more than just attraction though. I love him. I've never been in love before so I shouldn't know that's what this is; yet I do. My body buzzes all over simply being in the same room as him. My heart won't stop racing. My face flushes and my stomach churns like a thousand little dancers are moving in there.

What is going on?

"Morning, class. I am Professor Colin Read." His gaze pans around the room and stops when he spots me. He pauses as though shocked, and then continues as if everything is normal. "I'd like to thank Sarge for taking over the reins for the past couple of weeks."

I don't remember anything else he says for the entire lecture. Instead of listening, I watch him curiously, trying to figure out how this could be.

Nerissa pokes me in the ribs as we leave the classroom.

"Hey. Are you okay? You hardly said a word in there."

She's right.

I'd sat mesmerized by his brown eyes, soft face, and delicate mouth. I'd been unable to take my eyes off him, Colin Read, my university lecturer — the love of my life. I sat motionless and watched him.

This doesn't make any sense. *Ryder! What am I going to tell Ryder?* How am I going to explain it's over for a man I have never said a word to? I don't understand why or how, but I am in love with Colin Read.

What are you thinking? You're not in love with this man, and you are not breaking up with Ryder. Get a grip on yourself. It's probably another hallucination side effect thingy from your medication.

Maybe talking about it will help.

"Nerissa," I'm nervous of her reaction but continue, "Do you believe in love at first sight?"

There had been a moment between the professor and me, I'm sure of it. His eyes lingered on my face, widening in recognition. He knew it too. I resisted the urge to reach him after class, and thankfully, the choke of dissipating students stopped me from doing anything stupid. Before he rushed out the door, he stared at me again.

"Sure, in theory. I wouldn't be a good romance fan if I didn't. Why?"

I inhale and search for courage, but it fails me. "Never mind."

We walk in silence to the library and take a spot on a sofa chair that is nestled behind the non-fiction section.

"Have you decided what story you're going to use for the first assignment?" Nerissa's nose twitches from side-to-side as it does when she's contemplating things.

"Nope. How about you?"

"Thinking *Jane Eyre* and exploring the vampirism themes."

I acknowledge her robotically, searching for something to say, but my mind keeps slipping to Colin. His sandy brown hair, the way a dimple appears on his left cheek when he smiles, his velvety voice.

Oh my goodness. He has to be more than ten years older than me, at least. What if he's the same age as Dad? You're being like a reverse Mrs. Robinson. Cut it out.

This should creep me out way more than it is. What's wrong with me?

"Oh, how about you and Ryder come out with us this weekend? We can go uptown and do some dancing?"

"Hmmm, that could be good. I'll check what we're up to." Yet my thoughts morph from dancing with Ryder to swaying in Colin's arms, his hands holding me close. I shake my head, and the disturbing image dissipates.

"Hey, there you are." Nerissa's boyfriend, Dylan, runs his hand through his blond hair. With the way his short locks flow in miniature waves he could easily grow a golden afro.

"You found our hidey hole." Nerissa motions to me. "Dylan, you remember Mishca from school, right?"

Dylan squishes in beside Nerissa. His shoulders are so broad he takes up more than half the sofa. "Of course. Hey, Mish." He gives me a blank stare.

"I dobbed Dougie in for trying to perv up her skirt at school," says Nerissa.

He peers at me more intently, and the penny drops. "Don't take offense, Mish. He was a serial up-skirt offender." I don't appreciate the smirk. "Baby-cakes, we've gotta cruise. Remember, we have to be home for that thing."

Nerissa's face goes soldier stoic before she clicks her tongue. "Oh, yeah, the thing." I look at them like a stunned mullet, but they obviously have no intention of letting me in on it. Nerissa packs up her stuff, and they leave.

"See you in class," she calls over her shoulder.

I open up my copy of *Wuthering Heights* and contemplate how I can tie in something cool. *Ghosts are coming back. Maybe I'll focus on that.* No matter how hard I try, I have no empathy for Heathcliff. He needed to brush that chip off his shoulder and get on with his life instead of making everyone else's life a living hell. He took the whole revenge thing too far.

Even though I've read it all before at least twice, I start again from the beginning. I'm unsure if I'll remember enough detail to use for the assignment without going over it again. With my mind refusing to focus, I have to keep rereading pages.

"Hey, babe, here you are." Ryder strides toward me, tense shoulders relaxing at the sight of me. "I was worried something had happened to you when you were not waiting out front."

Boy, I'm a dumbass sometimes. "Sorry. I guess I forgot."

Ryder raises an eyebrow but says nothing and moves to go. Slowly, I gather up my things and follow.

"That looks heavy. Would you like me to take something?" He motions to my pile of textbooks.

"No, I'm fine." I'm glad to have my hands full. The last thing I want right now is to hold hands with Ryder. My head is all muddled up. I doubt physical contact with him will make it any better. Besides, I find the pile of textbooks as light as feathers.

We navigate through the labyrinth of buildings with Ryder trying his hardest to start a conversation. I resist every attempt, wanting to get home and be alone. I need some serious vegging time to work out what I'm going to do.

Ryder opens the car door. "How is your course going?"

"Good." I gaze out the window as he starts the car.

"Even your peace and conflict class?"

"Nah, that was boring. I'm going to pick up another course instead." Images of Colin at the front of a class and thoughts about what other courses he teaches invade my mind. I shake my head again as though that would make the unwanted ideas go away.

"Lucky you. My first-year subjects are set in stone. Constitutional law is boring me to tears." Until today Ryder made my heart flutter, but now it starts guilt spiders crawling inside me.

I don't understand it. How could it all change so fast?

We continue in silence until we're nearly at my place when Ryder pipes up. "Is everything okay, Mishca? You seem distracted."

"Huh, what? No, I'm fine."

"Are you sure? Have you been having more of those dreams?"

"They're still around." I try to shrug the conversation off.

Ryder keeps glancing at me as he drives. "Maybe you should talk to Dr. Thompson about them, if they are making you this tired and—"

"No, I'm fine," I lie, cutting him off. I have to figure out what's going on. *You know what's going on. You're in love with Colin Read. Let Ryder go.* My heart agrees, but my head doesn't. *Come on, you've just met this guy today. Ryder is something real. You cared about him. How could that stop? You have no idea what the go is with this other guy.*

"Okay, if you say so." My lie is not convincing.

Relief washes over me when we pull up to my house. I'm more than eager to escape from the car.

"Thanks for the lift. I've got a ton of uni work to do, so I'll catch you next time." I rush to get out the door.

Ryder's mouth turns down, and his shoulders sag. "Do you want me to pick you up tomorrow for class?"

"Nah, our classes are a bit out of whack tomorrow. Besides, Betsy needs to go out for a spin."

"Oh, okay. I'll give you a call tomorrow night." Ryder's chin drops. He turns away. But at the last second, he spins with a cheeky grin, grabs my arm, and leans closer so he can give me a kiss. I melt into him and for a brief moment there's no one else but the two of us. Yet when our lips part, the world goes to shit again.

Why? The word bounces around my brain, but I can find no logical reason.

"Bye." I watch him retreating down the stairs,

part of me wanting to rush to him, and the other part fighting the urge to rush to Colin.

* * * *

"Finally, I found you." Colin stands before me dressed in a dated-looking suit. It's like the ones Dad wears in the pictures from when he and Mum were younger.

"I was right here all along," I say. He grabs my hand and guides me to him. His face has fewer lines, and his hair's a little darker.

Cool sand tickles my toes. Oh, a beach. The sun is half-hidden behind the sea-laden horizon.

"Don't leave me. Don't ever leave me again. My life is nothing without you." He kisses me lightly on the lips.

"I'm not going anywhere." Our kiss deepens. I'm lost in him. The temperature around us drops. I shiver, pulling away. The sun has gone, and the stars twinkle down at us.

I turn to Colin, but he is no longer beside me. My eyes follow the footprints and find him farther down the beach. We try running to each other, but the gap between us keeps widening until he's a speck on the horizon.

"Colin!" My cry echoes throughout the night.

"I'm right here." His voice comes from behind me.

"Thank goodness!" I clutch him. *"I thought I had lost you."*

"Don't ever leave me." I recoil in horror. The voice isn't Colin's, but it is one I'm so familiar with now. The man with the long brown hair looms over me.

The sand beneath me begins to give way. I sink up to my knees. The stranger holds out his hand, but I can't reach him. Although he's standing still, he keeps getting further and further away from me.

"Colin! Colin, come back!" *I scream. Then, I realize someone else loves me and can help.* "Ryder. I need you."

The sand creeps up, burying half of my body. I try desperately to dig my way out until I am clawing so hard the grains of sand wedge under my nails. My flailing arms achieve nothing. As the sand reaches my shoulders, the man kneels beside me. "It doesn't have to be this way. I can take away your pain, your guilt. Come to me and I will make you my queen."

Self-preservation kicks in as the sand rises to cover my face. I try to reach for him. The man stretches to clasp my hand —

"Mishca, honey, wake up. Dinner's ready," Mum says, shaking me.

"Thanks, Mum. I'll be down in a minute." I put on my peppiest voice.

Once she leaves so does my smile.

CHAPTER 17

"HEY, NERISSA?" I tap her on the shoulder. I've been avoiding Ryder all week. My mind isn't getting any clearer. Everything signaled I was falling in love with Ryder, but those emotions are overshadowed by Colin. Every time I see him, my heart beats faster and my mouth goes dry.

"Yep." Nerissa glances up from her textbook. The grass in our little secluded patch behind the library is making me itchy. I fiddle with the Saint Christopher's key that Ryder gave me for Christmas and wonder how everything has managed to get so messed up since then. *You met Colin. That's how. And now, you love Colin.*

"You remember when I asked you if you believed in love at first sight?" I suck on my bottom lip and nip at it.

"Yeah, why?" That gets me a narrow-eyed stare.

I bite the bullet and spit it out because I need to talk to someone about it. "Because, I think, um, I felt it. Last week."

"Get out! What the f—! Mishca. I don't understand. What about Ryder? And who?"

I slump down and bury my face in my hands, the sobs rising. Nerissa touches my shoulder. "What's going on, Mishca?"

"I'm in love with Professor Read." *I love Colin Read.*

"I don't understand." Nerissa shakes her head.

"When I saw him, I can't explain it in a way that makes any sense. I knew I was in love with him. Like we were lost souls reunited." I pause, but Nerissa says nothing. "Oh Nerissa, what am I going to do? I still care about Ryder so much. Everything is so complicated now." I burst into tears and let her embrace me.

"Shhh, Mishca. It'll all be okay." She pats my hair soothingly. "You're probably just freaked about getting serious with Ryder. It'll work out. See Ryder this afternoon, have a good make out session, and this infatuation with Professor Read will disappear."

Suddenly, fury overrides the pain and sorrow. I push free of her arms and get to my feet.

"How dare you! You have no idea what I'm feeling! Just because you have no choice in your future doesn't mean this isn't real!"

I stomp away, my mind filled with a muddle of thoughts about Colin, Ryder, and Nerissa. I find an empty path and pace back and forth trying to calm down. My soul is pulled in every direction until I want to explode. I focus on the drinking fountain ahead, and rush at it, kicking with all my might. The metal creaks in protest. Then, it topples over with water spraying everywhere. I groan and attempt to put it upright but end up ripping it off its hinges. I throw it to the ground and dash away, hoping no one has seen the mess I've made.

* * * *

"Rough day, honey?" Mum wrinkles her nose as I try to dash through the kitchen to my room. She's not having any of that, though, and places her hand on my arm. I want to shoulder her away, but I don't want us back on eggshells with each other like we were before Christmas. Besides, I've pissed enough people off today. So instead, I pull out one of the bar stools and lean my elbows on the cool marble top. The kettle starts gurgling.

"You could say that." Her green eyes meet mine. "Uni stuff." I neglect to add I've fought with Nerissa. My jaw tightens as I replay the argument in my mind. On one hand, Nerissa let me down as a friend when I needed her the most; on the other hand, I behaved like a spoiled brat. I indulge Mum as she goes through her day, smiling and nodding when I should. I answer everything with the responses a good daughter would give. I need to do something right today. An hour later, I retreat to my room to tackle my uni work.

Flipping open my laptop, I try to focus on my literary assignment. We have to find common elements between one of our assigned books and modern trends. It's too easy to take an Austen classic that has been modernized, so I stick with my original plan of *Wuthering Heights* and ghosts.

The page remains blank for a few minutes before I type in some notes, and then I'm stuck about what to write. I don't particularly like *Wuthering Heights*, but it is well written. Most of the characters annoy me to no end. Some are victims of circumstance, but others could have made much better choices. It's almost incestuous at times with so many characters that have intertwining lives. I stand firm in my view that Heathcliff's a pig.

I get no further with my mind wandering between Colin, Ryder, and Nerissa, so I slip into Facebook, hoping inspiration will visit me at a later date. Some random friend requests are waiting for me.

Sorry, don't know you—ignore. Or you—ignore. The third one has a message. *Hey Mischievous Michelle—I finally found you on here!* I don't recognize the name, Toni Harrison. Then, I remember I've been mistaken for a "Michelle" on here before. Curiosity wants me to search for her to see if we do look that much alike, but I can't remember her surname. I decide to accept the friend request, hoping I might be able to find out more from this girl.

I contemplate sending Nerissa a text apologizing but can't find the right words.

Everything is so jumbled. How am I going to make it right? And what about Ryder...and Colin? I hate myself. And I hate Colin for stuffing up what I have with Ryder. *Why is this happening to me?* A horrible thought hits me. I haven't even spoken to this guy, and I think I love him. *Does this have something to do with my changes? Because this is not normal at all?* Then, I know what I have to do. I have to fight for Ryder. He's the one I'm meant to be with. Not some random man that my crazy mind thinks I love. My fingers flit over my phone, sending the text to Ryder. He replies, and after thirty minutes of torture, I'm at the front door, sneaking Ryder into the house.

"Hey you." I let Ryder's voice penetrate the defenses that have surrounded me all week. "Pretty excited to get your message. Are you sure this will be okay?"

I nod and pull him into the living room. "I had to see you." I didn't add that the need was to keep my sanity.

"Um, your dad is away, right?" He glances toward the stairs, leading to the family bedrooms.

"Ah ha. Mum's asleep." I wrap my arms around him and tilt my head back.

Ryder brushes my cheek with his fingertips. I shiver. His lips find mine and everything else in the world disappears. All I can think is about him, us, and everywhere we touch.

His hand slides down my neck, across my collarbone, and cups my breast. I arch my back, desperate to mold us together. My fingers find the hem of his t-shirt, and I yank at it. He creates space between us, enough for the material to slide past, and only pausing our kisses long enough for me to pull it over his head. His bare skin warms my hands as I explore his abs.

Why didn't I think of this sooner? In this moment, everything is perfect. All my doubts are gone. Ryder is the one.

My lips throb, but I don't care. Every inch of me vibrates under his touch. Ryder's lips trail across my jawline and move down my neck.

"I'm so sorry I've been weird," I whisper to the top of his head.

His teeth graze skin; then, he nips and murmurs, "Apology accepted, though you have nothing to apologize for."

I sigh and let him continue his nibbling.

Threat detected.

Shut up! I squeeze my eyelids tight and grasp Ryder even tighter, desperate for his body to cure me.

Does he know what an abomination you are? The familiar female voice taunts me.

Not now! I push my nails into Ryder's back and drag them down with measured force. He moans into my neck and softly sucks.

Threat imminent. Defensive mode initiated.

My body ignores my protesting thoughts and pushes Ryder off me. I spin around with fists raised and stare into my mother's bewildered face. The drink of water slides from her hands. Glass shards smash across the now wet floor.

"Sorry," says Mum in a strangled voice. "I was trying not to disturb you."

Ryder reaches for his t-shirt and crams it over his flaming face. He turns slightly as he gets redressed. The red scratch marks on his back show.

Mum raises an eyebrow but says nothing. I sigh.

"Ryder." Mum inclines her head at the door.

"Yes, ma'am." He kisses me chastely on the cheek, and then dashes off with a whisper of goodbye.

"Mum!" I make no effort to hide my mortification, though she doesn't realize that my reaction has to do with those voices in my head too.

"Mishca, I'm not going to scold you about Ryder. You know I understand. But something's not right with you." My insides squirm as she sighs. "I thought you would always talk to me, but I feel like you've put up a wall between us, and I don't know how to reach you."

I want to crack. I want to break down and tell her everything. But fear paralyzes me.

She exhales, strides over to me, and hugs me fiercely. "When you're ready. I'll be here."

I stay mute and still until she releases me and retreats upstairs. Once I hear her door click shut I slump onto the lounge, still warm with Ryder's body heat, and cry.

CHAPTER 18

NERISSA ISN'T IN CLASS. I'm not sure, but I get the feeling she's trying to avoid me. My gaze wanders around the room. The sight of Colin has me off guard, but I practice deep breathing from the mindfulness app Mum managed to sneak on my phone after the other night.

I watch him, mesmerized by his deep appreciation for my favorite authors and their works. He keeps peering at me too, eyeing me with a curiosity that simultaneously makes me want to snuggle up next to him and run into the safety of Ryder's arms. The whole situation unnerves me more than I want to admit. In a tutorial discussion, I speak to him for the very first time.

"So delving into a director's ability to accurately transpose classic literature from the written word to film, I would like everyone to think about their favorite movie adaption of a novel from our reading list and give me the reason it works."

That's easy. Participation in the tutorials makes up part of our marks for the subject, so I can't sit here and say nothing. I reluctantly raise my hand, and with the rest of the class still pondering the question, I get to answer. Colin acknowledges my opportunity to speak, but it's as though he's agreeing to it against his will.

"*Sense and Sensibility* with Emma Thompson. Apart from the story being a triumph of love over many obstacles, it shows us so much about the women of the time. We see them lamenting over the loss of their father but also their loss of status: the fact that they have to let some of their servants go, that they have to live in a house that is still bigger than a lot of people's houses today. It would be easy to focus on the absurdity of their plight by modern standards."

Says the poor rich girl.

"For me, the story is more about the importance of choice and the consequences, particularly for Willoughby. He let love go for the sake of money and social standing. Having to live with regret is a terrible thing, and the book and movie, portrayed this so well." I try my best to sound smart and polished. But I'm not sure if I pull it off because when I finish Colin simply stares. For a few moments, he says nothing until he notices the whole tutorial is watching.

Red-faced, he clears his throat, mumbles something in response, and then dismisses the class five minutes early. I'm at the back of the group of students stuck in the congestion as we all try to leave at once. My body ignores my internal protests and stops in front of his desk. It's been three weeks since I first saw him, first wanted to kiss his lips and call him mine, and three weeks since I wished I never laid eyes on him.

What are you doing? What about Ryder?

I ignore my inner voice and move forward.

"Excuse me, sir?"

The papers he'd been shuffling spill across the desk as he startles at the interruption.

"I'm Mishca, Mishca Richardson, and I wanted to say how much I'm enjoying your classes."

Shut up and run away, now!

Colin gapes at me dumbfounded and responds, "Yes, I know who you are." *Yippee.* "I mean, is there something else I can do for you, Miss Richardson?"

"No, sir," I mumble and make a hasty retreat.

My phone beeps up a message from Ryder. He's running late. I clutch the phone to my chest as though it'll infuse me with love for Ryder instead of Colin. *Maybe I do love Ryder and it's just different to what I feel for Colin. Maybe Colin is some bizarre infatuation.*

I stride toward the uni library, trying to rid my mind of my professor crush and concentrate on my boyfriend. I step inside the glass door, wrinkling my nose. The library has the most peculiar smell. I suspect one of the librarians is a germophobe as the odor consists of cleaning products. I settle into the corner at a coffee table and lounge combo, spreading out the reference books before me. I scour them for the information I need.

I scribble my notes, though my mind again flits between Colin, Ryder, and Nerissa. I pick up my phone, flick to my messages, and start typing one to Nerissa.

I'm so sorry. I was such an arse. Forgive me?

A couple of minutes later a new message pings on my phone. *Of course. Are you okay?*

That is the question of the hour. *Sort of.*

Then, he appears before me like a genie out of a bottle. If only he'd grant me the wish of not having feelings for him anymore. Colin rifles through a bookshelf to my right, apparently searching for something in vain. I watch him for five full minutes, memorizing the way his hair curls onto his collar, imagining the muscles flexing in his thighs as he squats to scour the lower shelves. Defeated, he flops onto a mini lounge meters away.

Slowly and deliberately, Colin turns toward me, as though he has now become aware of my presence. We study each other, like two long lost lovers reuniting, unsure where to begin. I move closer without making a conscious decision to do so.

"Hello, Professor Read. Do you mind if I sit with you?" Maybe if I talk to this man I can show myself this is a silly crush not based in reality.

I take his slacken jaw and lack of verbalization as a yes, though I struggle to work out what to say next. After some initial tension, the silence breaks.

"Miss Richardson," he inclines his head at me, "you said you're enjoying the course?"

I break out in a genuine smile. "Oh yes, very much."

"What has been your favorite part so far?"

"Definitely the Brontë sisters, though that'll be overtaken by Jane Austen when we get to it in full. *Pride and Prejudice* is my favorite."

Something softens in his eyes. "And why is that?"

"I'm not sure. Perhaps the triumph of love—the fact that Mr. Darcy is at first the ultimate bad boy who is tamed by the heroine—or maybe because of the happy ending."

Colin clears his throat, flips his wrist, and checks his watch. "It has been lovely talking to you, Mishca." My insides flip flop as he says my name. *Mishca, not Miss Richardson.* "But I have a prior engagement to get to. So until next class."

"Colin, before you go, I was wondering if you would like to catch up for coffee." The words are out of my mouth before I can stop them. *Where did that come from?*

Colin's face goes blank, and then simmers with hostility.

"Miss Richardson that would be inappropriate. You are my student." He makes his exit without another word.

I sit immobilized, staring at nothing. It *is* inappropriate, and my life is bad enough without some strange part of me trying to sabotage what I have with Ryder. I have to stop this. Now. Then, a little zap of inspiration hits. I march over to the administration center. A young receptionist puts on a plastic smile as I approach the counter.

"Can I help you?"

I nod. "I'd like to withdraw from my courses."

* * * *

"You did what?" Dad's voice booms off the white walls.

"I need some time to figure out what I want," I say. It's not a complete lie. I want Colin, but I also want Ryder. The only way to sort it out is to cut Colin out of my life completely. "So I thought I'd take another year off."

"Honey, why didn't you talk this through with us," says Mum, echoing Ryder's sentiments when I told him earlier.

"I suppose this is *your* influence?" Dad turns to my boyfriend.

"I had no idea Mishca was planning this. I am as shocked as you are," says Ryder with his hands raised in protest.

Mum glances at her watch. "We have to go. The Stevenson's party has already started."

"This discussion isn't over." Dad picks up his car keys. "Start thinking about a job because no daughter of mine is lazing around for a year."

I let free a sigh as my parents head out the door.

"And no funny business in my house," calls Dad before he slams the front door.

"That went okay," says Ryder, pulling me to him. "It could have been much worse. Why did you not talk to me about it first?"

"My mind was made up." I snuggle into his chest, trying to get lost in his embrace.

He picks me up and places me on the bench, wedging himself between my legs. His hand finds the nape of my neck, and he coaxes my head toward his. Our mouths meet, softly at first.

I move away. "Dad said no funny business," I tease.

"There is nothing funny about kissing you."

Maybe Nerissa was right, especially if the other night was anything to go by. Maybe all I need is a good dose of Ryder.

CHAPTER 19

THE MELODIC SONG of a magpie floats through the air. The crisp, cool morning is faking. It will be hot soon enough.

Ryder wraps his arms around me. I stare up at the rocky path we're about to climb. "Everything okay?"

I lie with a nod. Out of sight, out of mind isn't working as well as I'd hoped. I'm not thinking about Colin anywhere near as much, but he lingers on my mind like a stain that won't come out in the wash—you don't always see it, but when you do, you can't stop noticing it.

"Are we going to stand around here all day?" says Sophitia.

"Nearly ready," calls Nerissa, shoving the last of her supplies into her bag. She promptly passes it to Dylan to carry.

Yep, the bonding session between my friends and Ryder's friends is off to a great start. Ryder suggested that a hike would be a nice way to introduce our friends to each other. I'd prefer a barbeque, but once Finlay heard the idea, it was on.

"All right, let's go." Finlay springs up over the rocks. He's so graceful and does it with ease.

Connor, on the other hand, has legs and arms sprawling everywhere.

"Make way," yells Sophitia as she darts off and overtakes Connor.

Dylan and Nerissa set off next. Ryder and I follow close behind. The mixed terrain of dirt, rocks, and boulders provide little challenge, and I bounce across them with ease. It's not long before we've surpassed Connor as well as Dylan and Nerissa. The further up we get, the bigger the rocks until all we're climbing are boulders.

I reach up and grab a branch, planting my feet on the large rock and hauling myself up.

"And here I was thinking this would be a great excuse to hold your hand a lot — helping you up — but you are fine on your own," says Ryder, panting behind me. I turn, lie-down on the rock, and reach out my hand, grinning. "That fitness routine of yours sure must be working."

I pull my arm up, and he shoots through the air, arms flailing and expletives flying from his mouth.

He lands hard beside me. I glance around. *No one else saw.*

"What was that?" Ryder asks, his eyes wide.

"Is everything okay?" yells Finlay from a little farther up the path.

Nerissa and Dylan rush into view below.

"Everything's fine," I say.

Nerissa starts working her way up like I did with the branch but with significantly more difficulty. Finlay shimmies down.

"What is going on down there?" shouts Sophitia from up the track, a sharp edge of agitation in her voice.

"We will be there soon," Ryder calls back, keeping eye contact with me. He's clearly telling me this isn't over.

"Hey, a little help please?" calls Connor. He sounds like he's a good hundred meters behind.

Dylan's face pinches. "Hang on." He trots into the scrub below, disappearing from view.

Ryder, Finlay, Nerissa, and I all stand there with both the guys staring at me.

"What's going on?" Nerissa asks.

"Why don't you tell us, Mishca?" says Finlay, not stopping the glaring routine. "What *is* going on?"

Before I can respond, a loud crack splinters the air, followed by Sophitia yelling, "Look out!"

A boulder crashes through the scrub above. Everything moves in slow motion. There's no time to move, no time to push them out of the way. I rush forward and plant my feet, my elbows braced for impact. A grimace escapes me as the giant rock connects with my hands, my arms almost buckling. I manage to stand my ground. I squat down and spring up, aiming the boulder off to the right of my friends.

I wring my hands together, glancing around at the group while my stomach ties in knots. No more hiding the freak side now.

"Holy shit, Mishca," gasps Nerissa. "You saved us. How did you do that?"

"I don't know," I whisper. "Please, don't tell anyone. I don't want to be an outcast again. I just want to be normal."

"I knew it," exclaims Finlay. "I knew there was something funky about—ow." He rubs the spot where Ryder punched him.

"What is up here?" asks Ryder.

I take a deep breath in and exhale. "Ever since my operation I've been different. I can't explain why or how it happened. But I can do things. Like that. Although, I didn't quite realize how much like that." I gesture at the flattened shrubbery marking the boulder's path.

"Are you guys okay?" cries Sophitia, sliding down the rock face above. "The boulder shot out from under me, and I thought you were goners." She rushes over and flings her arms around Ryder. "I thought you were dead."

"We are fine," replies Ryder, stroking her emerald hair. But he's fixed on me.

Connor's flushed face pokes through as he scrambles over the rock. He raises an eyebrow at the odd scene—Sophitia in Ryder's arms and the rest of us off to one side in an awkward huddle. My boyfriend releases his friend and steps toward me.

Dylan comes into view. "Hey, guys. I found an easier walking trail over here. How about we take that one?"

We all nod and let him lead the way. Ryder keeps glancing over at me, the hurt evident on his face. *I kept this from him. And a lot more.* Guilt twinges inside me at my other secret.

CHAPTER 20

BEING DEAD AND coming back to life runs the risk of something from the other side crossing over with you. Even with a medically controlled death and revival like mine. At least that's what Nerissa theorized when we discussed my new attributes and what my friends witnessed firsthand a few days ago. When they all stared at me in horror, I started to wonder if she could be right.

Now comes the real test.

My hands come together without strain or sweat, bending the iron bar in my grip. I avoid eye contact with my friends, focusing instead on my shadow on the sand.

Nerissa does her best impersonation of a goldfish before closing her mouth. Her blue eyes plead with me. "You've got to entertain the idea now that you could be—"

"Possessed? Come on." Ryder runs his hand though his hair. Not that his theory is any better. Dr. Thompson is *not* some mad scientist who experimented on me.

The sun peeks over the bush-clad mountains that skirt the hidden beach. We're lucky Nerissa's parents have this holiday house, north of Brisbane. Hopefully, no one will see me being put through my paces.

Finlay places his pen against the clipboard. "Okay, so we know you're unbelievably strong. What do you want to try next?"

I shrug, tossing the iron bar on the ground. "I don't know. What else is on your list?"

"Hearing and speed are obvious ones," he replies. "So how about one of those?"

"We could do them together if you run to the end of the beach, and then wait to find out if you can hear us?" suggests Ryder.

"Sure," I reply.

Nerissa clicks on the stopwatch. "Ready? Go!"

My muscles tense, coil, and then spring to life. The wind whips around me, and in seconds, I'm at the other end of the beach. I pause, waiting for the old pain in my chest to start up, but it doesn't. My eyelids scrunch as I try picking up distant voices.

"How far was that?" Ryder's words come though like an echo down a tube.

"Maybe two hundred meters?" replies Finlay. "It's more than the length of a footy field."

"What's the sprint world record?" pipes in Nerissa.

"Not as quick as that," says Ryder with a twinge of concern. "Do you reckon she can hear us?"

"If she can, she'll know I think Ryder would like some superhuman loving tonight," says Finlay, laughing.

"Eww. Could you be any more crass?" says Nerissa.

I snort then relax and let their voices drain away. I jog toward them. That's the farthest away I've been able to eavesdrop. It's been hushed whispers I've picked up so far. It's not something I get all the time anymore, mainly only when I want to, thank goodness.

"Could you hear us?" asks Ryder once I'm closer.

I nod, shooting Finlay a dirty look.

"She heard me all right." He laughs again.

"How do you block it out? I'd go insane hearing everything all the time." Nerissa makes no attempt to hide her apprehension.

"It doesn't work like that. It's like I tune in on conversations." I try to reassure her.

"I wonder if you could hear me through the trees," says Finlay as he starts up the beach, flinging his folder in the sand. "Wait a few moments, and then listen."

"Are you okay?" Nerissa surveys me from top to bottom.

"Sure. Who doesn't like being a human guinea pig?" I shrug with false bravado. She swoops in and embraces me. I sigh. "I'm sick of being different."

"You know that doesn't matter to me."

I nod into her shoulder. She releases me, smiling, and I can't help but grin back.

"Can you hear that knucklehead?" Ryder looks up into the foliage that hedges the beach.

I drop Nerissa's hand and lean forward. "Nope, not a peep." I wait a bit more, and when I still can't hear Finlay, I call to him, "Okay, you can come out now!"

"What's he playing at?" Nerissa huffs and taps her foot.

I dash up the sand, following his footsteps, but pause when I reach the vegetation. Most of the grass is curving to the right with the breeze, but there's a small line that's bent to the left. I follow that line as it veers off in a crocked path, the grass replaced with dirt and rocks. Up ahead, a freshly spun spider web hangs limp, broken. I make a beeline to it and continue as I see small rocks overturned, their dark bellies showing where they've been kicked free of the dirt. Suddenly, there are no signs of previous movement. I stop in my tracks, surveying my surroundings. Bark on the ground at the base of a tree. On the trunk is a bare patch.

"Come down, Finlay." I don't even bother looking up.

"Good at tracking too, eh," he says as he shimmies down.

"I guess."

We walk in silence until we reach the others. Finlay picks up his board and writes.

"Care to share?" Nerissa asks.

"I stayed quiet. I wanted to see if she could find me," he replies. "And she did. The girl's got tracking skills too."

"I guess no one will want to play hide-and-seek with me anymore," I snap.

"Did you ever do karate?" asks Finlay.

"No," I respond, cocking my head at him as he puts his stuff down.

"Surely your parents would have gotten you to do self-defense classes," he continues, taking a few steps in my direction until we're an arm's length apart.

My skin prickles. I watch him. Without warning, he throws a right hand punch at my head. I sidestep, grab his wrist, and snake my arm around his until it's locked in. Eyes narrowed, I hyper-flex his arm up, almost to the breaking point, until he groans with pain and taps his leg. I stay still. Behind me, Ryder and Nerissa are yelling for him to cut it out and for me to release him.

"I'm tapping out, Mishca," he gasps. "It means I yield. You can let me go."

I ease off the pressure and start to unwind my arm. Before I've released him fully, he swings a left. My hand catches his fist. I clench my fingers. I sweep out his legs with a swift kick, and then jump on his chest, pinning his arms with my knees. I strike at his face, stopping my hand millimeters from his cheek.

"Oh, I like this position." Finlay grins. "Maybe I should jump you more often."

"Oi!" cries Ryder, lifting me off his friend.

"So what was that all about?" I brush the sand off my knees as I wait for an answer.

"I wanted to see if you could fight. You've never had any training, yet you instinctively took me down."

"And so easily," chimes in Nerissa.

Finlay pulls a face as he gets to his feet. "We've forgotten one."

The rest of us whip our heads toward him. He stares at me. It's obvious he no longer sees the stuck-up rich girl he thought I was when his mate and I started dating a couple of months ago. I was so scared when the three of them saw me catch the boulder that they'd be spooked. But they've got a fascination with me now that seems to be preoccupying them.

"What?" asks Ryder.

"Do I have to spell it out? She's like a female Superman. We haven't even gone through all the powers."

The image of me in spandex flashes through my mind. With my almost-afro, caramel skin, and almond-shaped eyes, I'd make a pretty kick-arse cartoon hero.

I peer at Ryder. While my boyfriend is in my sights, my mind starts drifting to Colin. Tearing my gaze from his face, I concentrate instead on his clothes, trying to push away any other thoughts.

"Nope, no X-ray vision," I say.

This gets me a wink instead of a blush. "Such a shame too." Ryder lifts up his T-shirt to show his ripped abs. "But all you have to do is ask if you want to see me out of my clothes."

I can't help but grin.

"We can cross off heat vision too," says Nerissa, pulling her blond hair into a makeshift ponytail. "Mishca was staring so hard Ryder's clothes would have spontaneously combusted if she had that power."

Finlay shakes his head. "You guys are missing the obvious one." He pauses as though for dramatic effect.

"Hell no." I fold my arms.

He could be taking the Mickey out of me. It's always hard to tell with him.

"Lots of supes are aliens. Maybe you're an alien."

I want to punch that Roman nose right off his face.

"I'm not an alien." It's true I don't know who my real parents are. But I've got a birth mum and father somewhere, and I'm going to find them.

"Prove it." Finlay folds his arms. "Try and fly."

"Come on, mate," starts Ryder, but I signal to him that it's okay.

"Fine."

"This is crazy," says Nerissa in a shrill tone.

"Not as crazy as me being possessed," I shoot back with a wry smile.

I retreat a few steps and zero in on the rocks at the end of the beach. My legs start to pump, building up speed. I jump, the air rushing past my face. Stretching my body into the conventional flying position, I try to guide toward my goal. It takes a couple of seconds before my face meets the ground and I'm eating sand.

Spitting the grains out of my mouth, I glare at Finlay, who's now doubled over with laughter. Ryder rushes over to me with Nerissa in tow. Their mouths twitch like they're caught between concern and amusement.

"Are you all right?" He helps me brush off the sand, and then glares at his friend.

"Yeah, I'll be fine."

"You're bleeding," cries Nerissa.

I pluck the sunglasses from Ryder's head and inspect the wound in the reflection. A gash trickles blood down my face like a tiny red river. I walk over to our stuff, grab a towel, press it to my head, and then check the time. It's almost seven in the morning. The plan was to stay here longer, but I'm not in the mood anymore.

"That'll do for now." I check my injury again. It's still bleeding. I turn to Finlay. "It appears I can't fly *or* heal."

He looks away sheepishly.

The four of us head to Ryder's car.

"We're going to need to work out why this is happening to you," Nerissa starts as she stoops to get in.

"I don't want to deal with it anymore today," I say through gritted teeth.

The three of them say nothing and seem to respect my need for private thought. I've barely been able to think about anything but my changes since I started noticing them not long after my operation.

"Huh?" Ryder had been talking to me, but I didn't catch what he'd said.

m glad you let me in. I know you do not want to think about it anymore today. But I needed tell you that." He reaches over and squeezes my hand, glancing at me before watching the road again. There's something in his eyes, like he's keeping something from me. He's probably more shaken than he wants to let on.

I give him a weak smile and try to convince myself that it's a good thing my friends now know about my strangeness.

CHAPTER 21

"THANKS SO MUCH for coming with me." I squeeze Ryder's hand. I rub my nose at the sterile smell of hospital.

"Not a problem." His smile lights up the room. "I know how much you hate being here. Besides, the Fitness Factory can last one day without me."

He glances at his watch. We've been waiting half an hour already for my appointment with Dr. Thompson. But I'm able to breathe and think rationally for the first time in a long time. I have to push aside whatever infatuation I have with Colin. What I've got with Ryder is real and strong. We care for each other. And he hasn't run for the hills in seeing who I really am.

But you don't love him like you love Colin. My mind refuses to let go.

Shut up!

Ryder twitches in his seat. He never likes to sit still long, but then again, neither do I. And we've got somewhere else to go after this.

"So is it anything major?"

"No, a routine checkup." I pause, and then add, "And Dad thinks I should tell Dr. Thompson about those dreams I keep having."

"Probably a good idea. Are you going to tell him about the hallucinations too?"

I shrug.

Ryder strums his fingers against his leg.

"Are you okay?" I ask.

He reaches a hand up and rubs his neck. "Got to go," he inclines his head toward the toilets, "you know."

"Sure. I'm going to stretch my legs anyway."

"Be back in a minute."

I watch Ryder head down the hall before walking to the edge of the reception room. Dr. Thompson's office is near the hospital chapel. Last time I was here, I heard that creepy conversation and met the priest. It might be nostalgia, but I find myself inching toward it.

An odd prickling takes over my toes and travels up my body, like the last time I was here. I peer inside the chapel.

It's empty.

I step in, my fingers brushing against lily petals in a flower arrangement near the door. The odd sensation intensifies. I walk forward to the windows and gaze at the gargoyles on the ledge. The warrior one catches my eye like before, but it must be a new statue as it's in a different position.

I look up at my reflection in the window with so many thoughts swirling through my head. Colin, Ryder, all the weird stuff that's been happening, my birth parents. I squeeze my eyes shut, trying to empty my mind. When I stare at my reflection again, I see double. The second me grins and slices her finger across her throat.

"You're so dead," says a voice like mine, hot breath on my neck.

I whip around to an empty chapel. The flowers in the vase at the entrance sway. I rush to the hallway, but no one's there, let alone someone like me. *Who am I kidding? I don't have a twin.* Something in the recesses of my brain reminds me that stranger things have been happening. And the reality is, I don't know. I never will.

I withdraw to the reception area, greeted by Ryder with his hands shoved in his pockets. He glances around but relaxes when he sees me. He waves a copy of a surgery-recovery pamphlet of the dos and don'ts for heart surgery patients in front of me.

"See anything interesting in there?" I ask, and then blush as I remember the contents of the brochure. Mum and I had gone through it before my operation. No alcohol, of course. I'm allowed to have sex—not that I've actually had any yet—as long as I don't overexert myself. The pamphlet recommends trying *new things* to make it fun and exciting. I had been able to tell when Mum read that part of the brochure because her ears went pink. It also lists the side effects of my medication, a wide range of physical and psychological ones are on the list and most of them quite gross. Depression, insomnia, anxiety—what a fun recovery! "On second thought, I don't know if I should let you read that. It might scare you off."

Ryder shakes his head. "Nothing could scare me off."

I push everything about Colin deep down inside because that's exactly what could send Ryder running for the hills. It's time to focus on what I have right here in front of me.

"Mishca Richardson," the receptionist interrupts us, "Dr. Thompson will see you now."

"I'll hold you to that," I whisper to Ryder as I walk into the doctor's office.

As much as I'd like my boyfriend in here to hold my hand, I also don't want the romance to evaporate with him thinking too much about me being cut open on the operating table. I need to get my love life back on track.

Dr. Thompson readjusts his glasses as I enter.

"Hello, Mishca. How's that heart of yours doing?" He asks that question every time.

"Still beating." I focus on the picture frame on his desk.

We go through the standard checkup until the point where he asks if I have any questions. I've never had any — Mum gathered enough information beforehand, making sure I was *fully* informed — so Dr. Thompson raises an eyebrow when I speak.

"Well, there is something," I start, not quite sure how to say it aloud. I opt for the direct approach, "I've been having these, ah, nightmares."

"Oh." He shifts in his seat. "What are they about?"

"Often they're about my heart transplant but sometimes they're horrid. People chasing me, trying to kill me, telling me what a bad person I am. Stuff like that." I have trouble meeting his eyes.

"Hmmm," he says taking some notes. "And how often do you have them?"

"Every night," I whisper. Clearing my throat, I raise my voice. "I thought it might be a side effect of the medication."

"Unlikely, but not out of the realm of possibility. Certainly not something I've come across before." He makes another note. "You've had them every night for all these months now? You should have brought this up sooner."

"And there's been hallucinations," I add. "I've seen myself, but it's not me. I may have had one now before I came in. The other me, she wants me dead."

His face softens. "Mishca, people are often faced with their mortality when they go through this type of surgery. Have you been going to a psychologist at all? Or a counselor?"

I shake my head.

"Then, maybe you should. You've been given a second chance at life. You should be enjoying it, not feeling guilty about being alive."

"Pardon?" His words hit too close to how the dreams make me feel.

"I would understand if you felt bad about someone else dying so you could live. But it's not like you killed them. They were a willing donor who knew that they would be helping multiple people improve their quality of life once they'd passed on."

He hands over a card. I take it and shove it in my bag.

"Was there anything else?"

A vision of me strapped to a table in a lab springs into my mind, followed by me in a straitjacket. I keep my mouth shut.

"No."

"Make yourself an appointment." I nod at his words. "Good. Now get out there and enjoy your life."

He always ends our sessions with that statement, so I take my cue to leave.

Ryder is dutifully waiting outside. I grab his hand and head straight for the exit. The doors slide open and the odor of antiseptic is replaced by fresh air laced with the scent of eucalyptus in blossom. I'm so glad to be out of the hospital.

"What did Dr. Thompson say about your dreams?" asks Ryder as he hops in the driver's seat.

"He said it was no big deal." I pretend to take an interest in something out the window.

"Right," he replies with a drawl.

I sigh. "My doctor is not an evil genius who experimented on me while I was under." He's been spouting that theory ever since he found out about my changes. I find it preposterous. Mad scientist human experiments went out with the Dark Ages, right?

"You never know, Mishca." He cracks a grin. "You just never know."

CHAPTER 22

I DRAG FREE OF another nightmare. The dreams don't have the same impact. Maybe I'm getting too desensitized to them. Either way, I'm not going to let them get to me. *Today is going to be a good day.* I repeat it like a mantra in my head.

It doesn't take me long to freshen up. I rifle through my wardrobe for something to wear. I push the coat hangers across and eye the cute dresses that I've been neglecting because they show my scar. I reach for one, hesitate, and then withdraw my hand. *Maybe not yet.*

"Mishca, breakfast is ready," calls Mum from the kitchen.

I gallop downstairs. "None for me. I'm having breakfast in the city with Ryder before work."

"Are you sure about that job? Working in fast food is so—" she cuts herself short. "I could get you a job at a magazine, or your father could have you working with his team, maybe in public relations or events."

"I'm going to enjoy working with Nerissa. It's fine. I'll be back at university next year," *one without a Professor Colin,* "so I don't want anything permanent. This is just a fun job for my gap year."

Two lines appear between her eyebrows with more across her forehead, but she says nothing.

"Where's Dad?"

"Early morning training with the team."

"Cool. Well, I'll see you tonight after my shift."

Even at seven in the morning, the Brisbane traffic starts to condense and public transport is even slower. But I don't want to be leaving Betsy in the city all day, and with Ryder pulling an all-night stock-taking shift at the Fitness Factory, there was no sense in him coming out of the city to pick me up. The bus rocks at each stop. I enjoy the swaying sensation. It takes less time than I thought to get to my stop. I trudge down the steps of the bus and look around. I don't see Ryder, and the bus stop bench is full, so I walk over to the building behind the stop and lean against the wall. So many women in dress suits and joggers power walk past as well as men in business gear.

Then, I see him. My heart skips a beat. *Colin.* He stops dead in his tracks on the footpath as I come into his view. The moment captures us both, and he's oblivious to the grumpy workers who have to veer around him. My heart beats an odd rhythm. *He kind of reminds me of a preppy Hugh Jackman.* My stomach does little backflips at the sight of him in his running gear, his t-shirt clinging against the muscles in his chest, his phone strapped on his bicep. His steps slow as he approaches me, and a confused look crosses his features.

"Miss Richardson, what are you doing here?"

"I'm meeting someone," I say, suddenly remembering Ryder.

"And you decided to camp out on my door?" His tone sounds almost accusing.

"Um, what?" I look around and realize that the wall I'm propping up against belongs to an apartment block. "Oh, you live here?" For some reason my mind scans the building number. Pain at once sears through my chest. I can't breathe. I scream. That tearing that I hadn't experienced in years is back, ripping me apart from the inside out. I slide down, ignoring the urgent questions from Colin.

He reaches for his phone, calling an ambulance.

"No!" I cry out. "No ambulance. I'll be fine," I manage to gasp, worried they'll find more than a heart transplant scar; something that will result in me being in a lab. "I've just got to ride it out."

"Are you sure?"

I nod. "Please, don't." Tears threaten to overwhelm me. With everything I've been through I don't need this old issue coming back.

He says something into the phone cancelling the ambulance. I focus on breathing to calm down.

"You dropped out."

"Huh?" I look up at him and lose count of my breaths.

"Of uni. I noticed you stopped coming to class, and then I saw you weren't in my classes at all anymore."

"Yeah, I was dealing with," I pause to find the right words to explain," some stuff."

That sounds so lame.

He reaches down to help me to my feet. We end up standing so close I can feel his breath dance across my skin. I could lean in and our lips would touch.

Stop it! What are you thinking?

My legs wobble, and I stumble into Colin. Then, my knees buckle. He catches me. My skin sears with heat at his touch.

Great, superpowers desert me at the worst possible time.

"How about you come in and rest?"

My mind wants to protest, but instead, I nod in ascent. He scoops me into his arms, bustling me through the lobby and into the elevator. I don't dare look at his face, knowing if I do I will likely want to pounce on him.

Think of Ryder. Think of Ryder's eyes. Think of Ryder's abs. Hmmm, abs.

At his door he places me on my feet, and I don't fall in a heap. Mesmerized, I watch him slip his key into the lock, turn his wrist, and lead me into his world. As I step over the threshold, I'm entranced. The apartment is small and neat with the exception of piles of books stacked in the oddest locations: on the mantelpiece, the window ledge, and a rather large pile on a chair. Everything about it is so familiar. The smell of leather, musky manliness, and peppermint invade my senses.

Anxiety seizes me. *I'm in a stranger's house. One that you think you're in love with. Get out, now.*

"I should go," I say.

As I turn to run, I slam into Colin. Our eyes lock, what I'd been trying to avoid, and sparks fly between us. It's so wrong, and yet, so right. His hand caresses my cheek. As soon as his skin touches mine a jolt goes through my body. It takes every inch of my self-control not to rip Colin's clothes off and throw him on the floor.

What's happening to me? Who is this guy? I have to find out.

"I love you, Colin. From the moment I first saw you, I loved you. Why? I need to know why," I whisper.

Colin drops his hands, eyes wide, his unsettled face mirroring the conflict inside me. "No, no, it's not...right. Go."

I stand rigid, trying to work out what the heck has happened.

"Get out. NOW!"

I race from the apartment, push through the emergency exit, and vault down several flights of the stairwell. I stumble onto the street like a crazy woman. Pushing against the building's exterior wall, I try to make sense of everything. *Why is this happening?* Then, my gaze connects with Ryder's. He beams and waves. I can't even force a smile. It's been more than a month since I've seen Colin, and all my reactions are still the same around him. And even worse, I've betrayed Ryder. I haven't cheated technically, but emotionally, I have. I need to get my shit together.

"Hey," his bright disposition morphs into concern. "What is wrong?"

"I can't do this." I throw my hands up.

"What do you mean?" He reaches for my hand. I snatch it away.

"Us. I can't do *us* anymore." Tears well in my eyes and my heart constricts as I say the words. I have to do this. It's not fair to him. "It's not you, it's me. I have something I need to sort out and I can't do it with you as...a distraction." I can't bring myself to tell him I almost kissed someone else.

"Mishca, no. I do not care about your gifts; in fact, there is something I have to show you that will make everything—" His hand reaches for me and I want to melt. But I move away. I have to stay strong.

"It's got nothing to do with my abilities. It's something else. I wish there was another way, but there's not. I need space right now. I can't be with you fully with this hanging over me."

"Okay. I will not push you. But I will be waiting for you when you have things sorted out." It's just like him to understand. It rips my new heart in two. He embraces me. I sob into his chest. It's more than I deserve.

After a minute, I calm and pry free of his arms. He kisses my cheek, and I turn away. The pieces of my life crack with the pressure, but I don't look back. I walk out of his life.

* * * *

"I don't understand," says Nerissa as she leans on the Super Sundaes counter. "Everything was going so well."

"I almost kissed Colin."

"Oh."

"I can't explain it, but when I see him I can't control myself." I push the dishcloth around on the counter, not cleaning anything in particular. "You don't hate me, do you?"

She shakes her head. "I can't say I'm cool with it, but I think there's something else going on here. Do you think he's got something to do with your thing?"

"I'm not sure what you're getting at."

"Well, you have the dreams with some guy who says you're his, and then you see Colin and supposedly fall in love with him the moment you see him."

"Supposedly?"

"What if it's not real love? What if he's invading your dreams and making you fall in love with him?"

"That sounds like a plot for a bad novel."

"Sometimes life is stranger than fiction." Nerissa looks off, avoiding my gaze.

"You seem to be so willing to accept the strange and unexplainable."

Nerissa shrugs. "I think there's more out there."

She starts to uncover the ice cream containers in the display case, and then whips around to me. "Mishca, do you know whose heart you have?"

I stand still, staring at her. At first it was something that bothered me, before the heart transplant. But once it was beating in my chest, I never gave it a second thought.

"No," I say. "They never told me and I never asked."

"What if it belongs to someone who loved Colin?" She taps her index finger against her lips.

I frown. "It's just an organ. It's not like that's where the soul resides. Why can't you accept that I love Colin, and I need to see where this could go?"

"Because I don't buy it." She lifts the tub of sprinkles into the display case.

"So you accept your best friend has superpowers but not in love at first sight?"

She sighs. "Something like that."

* * * *

Dad walks in through the door, stinky from training, as the kettle clicks off. "You dumped Ryder? That's too bad. I was starting to like that kid." He heads straight for the fridge and grabs a bottle of water.

"Tom!" Mum gives him dagger eyes to match her tone, which softens when she speaks to me again. "You guys were going so well. What happened?"

"Well, I—"

"He didn't try anything funny, did he?" Dad cracks his knuckles and looks as though he's enjoying the thought of connecting them with Ryder's face.

"Dad, no! I, well, my feelings changed." *I love two guys at once, and I almost kissed the one I wasn't with, that's all*. I mentally berate myself for the callousness of my betrayal, but I can't seem to shake the other man. My whole body tingles just thinking about Colin and I drop my head ashamed.

"Well, you're still young," Mum says. "Give yourself some time to heal."

"Yeah, you know, there's plenty of fish in the sea and all that. Ow!" Mum's slim frame gives her a nice pointy elbow to shove into Dad.

Great pep talk, Dad. I make an excuse about being tired and head to my room, wanting nothing more right now than to be alone.

CHAPTER 23

MUM AND DR. THOMPSON must be on the same wavelength, because after finding out I broke up with Ryder, she booked me in to see her psychologist, Dr. Usher. I sit on the couch the whole time barely saying a word. When I exit the office, I go over all the things I didn't want to talk about. I've got unexplainable feelings for a guy old enough to be my dad. I cheated on Ryder. I could end up in a lab if people knew the truth about my abilities or a mental ward for my hallucinations.

I slam the key into my car lock and drive aimlessly, trying to shake off the building anger at the suckiness of my life. The last three weeks have been hell. My fists clench around the steering wheel. I have to keep control so I don't wrench it out of place. Suddenly, I'm outside the community hall of the adoption support group. I never wanted to go there again, but I could do with a distraction.

Betsy hums as I pull into the parking lot. I check my reflection in the rearview. Well, it's now or never. I scan the parked cars and assure Ryder's isn't there.

I stride to the door, head held high. *Things like this happen all the time. They won't judge you.* But I have my doubts. When I open the door to the community center, a wave of silence washes over the people in the know—Connor, Jamal, Trista. They all stop and stare while others who are oblivious continue on.

"Hey Mishca, long time no see." Trista bounds over, recovering first.

"It hasn't been that long." *Just a few months. Defensive much?*

Her red hair bounces around as she shrugs in response and heads to her seat. I hesitate, unsure of what to do. The red mass moves again when Trista jerks her head at the seat beside her. Jamal and Connor move away, distancing themselves from us both. They aren't hostile, just hesitant. It doesn't take long to find out why. Ryder comes through the door, head down, shooting pangs of guilt to my core...and something else. *Loneliness.* I miss him. The sensation hits me like a freight train.

He stops inside the door at the sight of me. His face clouds with hurt and bewilderment. With a word, he spins on his heel and leaves.

* * * *

I return home deflated. It doesn't make any sense to me. Seeing him tonight still hurt, but what he and I had was completely ruined by my feelings for Colin. It doesn't add up.

I grab my bag from the car and head upstairs. Mum and Dad are out on the deck and don't notice me slip by. I'm too shaken, so I head for the seclusion of my room.

Threat detected. I pause at the intrusion in my mind. Then, shake it off.

Yeah, yeah robot voice. Go tell someone who cares.

I'm shocked to find Sophitia sitting on the end of my bed. She beams, which is odd, considering the reception I've received from her to date.

"Hello, Mishca. I hope you do not mind but your parents said I could wait here for you."

I shrug in response but eye her. Today she is in a purple tartan skirt with knee-high black socks and ankle boots. She's also wearing a tight *Emily the Strange* black single top that shows off her assets. Her luscious green hair falls across her shoulders when she moves forward, leering at me.

"I heard you and Ryder are no longer paired."

"You heard right." *So you can move right on in,* I think with a twinge of regret.

"Are you with anyone new?"

I move my head slowly back and forth. *Why does she want to make my life so miserable?*

"Do you want to be?"

Her gaze is almost hypnotic. I respond as though under compulsion, nodding my head. Without warning, her mouth lands on mine. Her lips are soft like rose petals. I taste spearmint as she parts my lips with her tongue. Images of Colin and Ryder flash in my mind.

No, no, no, no, no.

This is wrong. It's not what I want. I manage to pry myself from her grasp and slide from underneath her, scuttling over to my study chair.

I regain my breath and turn to Sophitia. She stretches on her side on my bed, propped on her elbow, her head cradled in her hand. Her eyes, however, are not calm. They're no longer green but blaze with purple. I blink and they're green again. *Weird.*

"Wait, aren't you interested in Ryder?" I blurt out.

Sophitia throws her head back in gales of laughter, wiping away the tears. "Ryder! Why would I be interested in Ryder? My interests may not be mainstream, but I am not into kissing cousins."

A jolt of comprehension blazes through me. Ryder has been searching for his family, well his mother, and here's his cousin. "By blood?" I ask. She nods. "Does he know?"

She shakes her head. "When we learnt of him, my kin asked me to watch over him. Nothing more.

They forbade me to tell him anything. The journey to discovering who he is, he must travel alone. You must promise me you will not tell him."

Even though I don't owe her anything, I seem to run on autopilot, nodding. "I'll keep quiet for now. But you have to tell him." I pause, and then add, "He only talks of his mother. He never mentions wanting to find his father."

Sophitia picks at a piece of fluff off my bed. "I am not surprised." She doesn't elaborate, and instead changes the topic. "I wanted you from the instant I saw you. There *is* something about you, something special, so innocent and pure. Not normally my type." She winks and smirks. "Not that I have a type. Male or female, it is the person that attracts me."

She moves forward, kneeling in front of me, her head tilted to my face. She places her hand on my breast, not to cop a feel, thankfully. My skin prickles and heat spikes where she touches me.

"This is not your heart. How can you be sure of your emotions and desires when you love with a heart that belongs to someone else?"

My face becomes flush. I spring from my chair. *Maybe Nerissa is right. Maybe my new heart is taking over.* I pace my room, lost in thought. *Don't be stupid. Remember all those other ridiculous theories people came up with. This is just another one.* I waver. *Weirder things have happened to you.*

I brush away the intrusive ideas and settle on science. "It's an organ. It pumps blood. It's not a soul." My anger rises as I rummage around in my brain for the words, but the words fail me so I move to the door. "Okay, you've had your fun. Please leave. I'd like to be alone."

Gracefully, she rises from the floor, straightens her clothes, and begins to head out.

"Be careful. You are not wholly Mishca. Someone else is a part of you. You delude yourself to believe otherwise." Her face softens as I bend my head to hide threatening tears. She reaches forward and tucks some loose strands of hair behind my ear. I yield. That's all it takes, and Sophitia grabs the opportunity to brush her lips against mine. This time she intentionally cops a feel, and then darts out, throwing a mischievous grin over her shoulder. I groan and move to retreat into some Jane Austen for comfort.

It's then I see Mum standing in the hallway, mouth agape, chocolate chip cookies in hand. *Ahhh, crapspackle.*

CHAPTER 24

I WALK THROUGH the community center, groping in the dark, inching along until my legs connect with something hard — a chair. I sit in it, wondering where everyone else is. A soft light glows above me. Slowly, people begin to emerge from the darkness and move toward me. I can see Trista's red hair, Connor's pale face, Jamal's outline, and Ryder with his eyes flashing purple.

"What are you doing here?" hisses Jamal.

"You have no right to be here anymore." Trista waves a hand at the door.

"You gave up on your birth parents," Connor says harshly. "You gave up on Ryder."

The three of them move closer as Ryder hangs back. The eerie glow reveals grey, rotting faces. Their fingers point at me accusingly.

"You are no longer my Mishca. You are no longer his. You are no one's." Ryder's voice drifts over the top of the crowded ghouls. "You are guilty of betrayal; you are guilty of deception; you are guilty of lies."

The hands no longer point but move in to wrap around my neck.

"See." *That horrid voice is in my ear again.* "I told you there is no one but me. Come to me, I am waiting. I will take away the guilt, I will take away the pain. I will take you away."

"No!"

Reliving the torturous meeting in my dreams sucks. I wipe away the sweat, sitting in silence, still feeling the accusing eyes on me. He was at the adoption group first. Ryder has ownership of that territory. I have no right to go there. I've hurt and betrayed him enough. I decide it's best to get my mind off it. All I've got left now is work. In an ice cream shop. *Go me.*

So tired, I get up, bleary-eyed, and head into the bathroom. I grab at the handle and accidently push too hard. *Crack.* I groan, peering around at the damage. A squished doorstopper and a handle imprint on the wall.

Great start to the day.

* * * *

Two-and-a-half turns, twist, and the tip. My new ice-cream making mantra. Can my life get any worse? Mum and Dad still haven't been able to let it go that I've dropped out of uni and work at Super Sundae. The last month has been lonely with just Nerissa, the only friend I've been able to count on. And now my parents are adding the cost to repair the bathroom wall to my board. At least they accepted my explanation that I ran and fell into the door, though they did look skeptical.

"Would you like sprinkles with that?"

The woman shakes her head. *Sprinkles? What was I thinking? You offer that to kids. I should have offered choc dip.*

Nerissa glances over, giving me a quick wink as she moves to make a milkshake. Somehow, she manages to emanate springtime in her bright orange Super Sundaes uniform, whereas I resemble an overcooked dumpling.

"Hey, whatcha doing Friday night?"

A shrug is all I can muster. I'm starting to miss going on dates, and I am missing Ryder more and more. Then, I scold myself as though I am being unfaithful to Colin. *Unfaithful? How can you be unfaithful to someone you are in a one-sided relationship with? Someone who you don't even really know! And the one you were unfaithful to was Ryder!*

"Well, some of us are going dancing."

"Nixie and Douglas have 'broken up' and are 'seeing other people' at the moment." Nerissa uses her index and middle fingers to add the quotation marks. "So why don't you come along? Dougie might be the one to take your mind off everything."

I pull a face. The last thing I need is more guy complications. "I don't know, Nerissa, wouldn't that be weird? Going by what you said, you guys always end up back with 'the one'." I mimic her finger movements.

Nerissa raises a delicate shoulder, and then lets it fall. "Mishca, sometimes it's about fun. There's no need to make it more complex than life already is."

"Sure, okay. But I'm not promising you anything, except that I'll turn up and shake my booty."

"Great, you can be the DD."

I'm not sure whether I should be mad at automatically being the designated driver. Did she want me along or is it convenient because I won't be drinking? I brush it off. She'd want me there regardless, so whatever.

"Text me the time once you've worked it out." Nerissa is as disorganized as I am. I glance at my watch. "Hey, that's my break. I'm going to head off for tea. There are only so many times I can stomach hotdogs."

* * * *

I stare wistfully at the autumn collection in the window of a shoe shop. Dad and Mum figure as I'm nineteen they can't ground me, but they can take away my allowance and charge me board. That leaves very little money for shoes. I take a step forward to touch the glass as though it will allow me to walk through and make a gorgeous pair of heels mine. I stop mid-step.

Staring back at me is me, but not me in my horrid orange Super Sundaes uniform. It's me in black, looking leaner, harder, and stronger. The *me* in the window smirks and wiggles her fingers before turning her hand around in the shape of a gun and mimicking a firing motion.

I scan the area to see if anyone else is as shocked as I am to see my twin in the window, but when I turn back, there's just me in orange. Taking a step, I lean my hand and forehead against the cool glass, exhaling. Dr. Thompson wants to know if I hallucinate again, and now I can tell him I have. After being motionless for several minutes, I summon the strength to return to work when a tapping on the glass makes me jump. The shop assistant stares at me. A scowl is planted on her round face, and she calls through the glass, "Hey, get off. I'll have to clean that."

I wave weakly and mouth, "Sorry," before scurrying back to work.

* * * *

"Psst, Mishca." Nerissa crouches on the floor with a handful of lollies swiped from the decorations section. I duck down beside her and relieve her of a few, shoveling them into my mouth in the hopes of finishing them off before our next customer comes, or worse, our uptight boss, Jonathon. He's notoriously strict with the rules about not sharing food purchased with a staff discount—not even a sip of a shake is to be shared with friend or family at the risk of job termination. Personally, I think he suffers from short-man syndrome.

"Excuse me?"

I start to giggle but freeze—that voice. Elbowing Nerissa is useless. She shoves the remaining handful into her mouth, leaving me, still chewing, to respond. With a grimace on my lips, I get to my feet to face the person I both love and dread.

"Mello mir mhat man mi met mou moday?"

Colin's face scrunches into a perplexed frown. I swallow hard to get the remaining chocolate and candy shell down. "Pardon?"

"Sorry about that," I mumble. "What can I get you today, *sir*?"

The memory of him, yelling at me to leave his apartment like the whole thing was my fault, still stings.

"Hello, Mishca." His voice echoes soft and sorrowful.

Oh, please don't. I've been so strong. Don't torture me.

"What'll it be?" I blurt out.

Colin bites his lip, and somehow, I know that means something isn't going to plan. *But how? How can I know that?* I've seen him around. Most of the time he looks away, but sometimes I catch him staring.

"Um, can I please have a hotdog with cheese, mustard, and chili sauce?"

Strangely enough, I mutter under my breath, "You can, but will you?" Ryder is still there, a part of me. A pang of regret washes over me. I should have been courageous and told Ryder everything. *I still could be courageous and tell Ryder everything. What is wrong with me? Do it.*

"Pardon?"

"Nothing," I reply hastily, shaking my head at my own stupidity. "Coming right up."

Anger rolls through me for no apparent reason. Perhaps these delightful mood swings are brought on by the combination of my meds and the charming nightmares. I shove the roll onto the hotdog spike so hard it tears through the end. Normally, that'd warrant a new one, but Colin can suffer.

As I wait for the roll to finish on the toasting spike, I decide to be stingy with the butter/cheese spread, but heavy handed with the mustard and chili. *I hope you choke, you lovely bastard.*

Okay, and where did that come from?

It's like there are two of me fighting in my head. And it's totally exhausting.

"You can get that in a deal with a drink for an extra two dollars," I say automatically, "Well, two dollars for a can of drink or three dollars for a milkshake or small thick shake."

"Umm, no, that's fine. Look. In truth, Mishca, I'm not even hungry. I wanted to see you."

I ignore the smell of burning bread and the not-so-subtle peering of Nerissa. The anger subsides, but all I can do is stare.

"Could you meet me after work?"

"I could, but would I?"

"Sorry. Would you meet me after work?" He doesn't even bat an eyelash.

Mouth open and brows raised, Nerissa stays rooted on the spot before regaining control of her face. Colin is still a touchy subject between us. I can sense she wants to hit me with a, *"You must be kidding?"* But she stays silent.

"I don't think so." She's right. Seeing Colin would be the worst move ever.

"Mishca, there's something going on between us. I tried to fight it. But I can't stop thinking about you. Please, talk to me." The pleading in his voice matches the scenarios I'd played through my head thousands of times when I wanted to talk to him.

"I can't." I turn away and slip into the back room, leaving Nerissa to deal with my mess.

Nerissa is on the Team Ryder bandwagon, along with Mum and Dad. I guess they see him as a better alternative to my current misery. I wait for her to tell me it's all clear.

A few minutes later, she pokes her head through the door. "He's gone." She smiles at me weakly. "You did the right thing."

"Did I? This could've been my chance to determine what's happening." I squeeze so hard on the tomato sauce bottle that red goo splatters across my face.

Nerissa bursts out laughing, grabs some paper towels, and starts wiping my face. "Mishca, you know that I love you to pieces. You're my best friend, so whatever you want to do, I'll be here."

I wrap my arms around her, giggling, rubbing sauce on Nerissa. She squeals and tries to move away, but my grip stays firm.

"Umhm." A gruff throat clearing behind us makes us spring apart. Jonathon gapes at us with a mixture of disapproval and lust. *Oh great, just what I need, more fuel to add to the fire and make everyone think Mishca likes girls.*

CHAPTER 25

AS I PULL UP to Nerissa's house, I'm apprehensive for what will happen. I hope she made it clear I am emotionally unavailable. On second thought, I hope she's made it clear I am physically unavailable as well. Douglas slides into the car first with a grin of anticipation that heightens when he sees me.

I grimace.

Nerissa follows, looking apologetic, while the remaining three members of our group laugh and joke without noticing at all. I'm surprised at Nixie, who doesn't seem to care that Douglas has his eye on me tonight, despite their betrothed status. On the surface they seem like a great match, as all in Nerissa's group do. They're all tanned and various shades of blond.

Nerissa simmers down as Dylan nuzzles her ear before whispering something that makes her blush. Dorian, Nerissa's twin, has his arm slung around his girlfriend Nerine's shoulder and narrows his gaze at me with his sea-green eyes. I get the distinct impression he's not happy his sister has found a best friend outside of the clique, and seeing as we've already had one major falling out—over a guy—I'm obviously someone to keep an eye on.

"So where to first?" I kick the engine over.

"The Bowl," comes the unanimous chorus in reply.

It doesn't take us long to get into the city. Most people use public transport to avoid parking on the street at night, but Nerissa has teed up free parking at the Bowl's underground garage.

As we round the corner from the garage stairwell, I groan. The queue is huge. Apparently, though, that's not a problem. Nerissa marches to the front of the line, Nixie in tow, and taps a giant Samoan man on the shoulder.

"Hello, Nerissa. I see you are already on the guest list so why don't you come on in."

A chorus of groans emanate from the line of waiting patrons. We walk through the door and I get an eyeful of Nerissa as she strides in front of me. She isn't in her usual Bowl attire which consists of anything black and slinky. Instead she's wearing a bright blue sequined dress—still slinky—that matches the interior décor and strappy silver shoes.

The whole group is breaking dress code. Douglas dons all white. Nerine and Dorian are each wearing shimmering silk tops that change from blue to green depending on the light. Dylan is in a navy blue suit with a white tie, and Nixie is in a flowing pink dress with gladiator heels. Me—I'm in a simple black mini dress with my latest pumps that took me a whole month to save for.

As we make our way in, I see everyone's wearing masks. The young party hostess at the door kisses each person in our group on the cheek before handing them a mask. A white furry tiger mask goes to Douglas, a silvery-blue mask with a pattern like scales to Nerissa, and a similar deeper blue mask for Dylan. Matching peacock masks are handed to Dorian and Nerine and a pink butterfly mask for Nixie.

The hostess kisses me next and shoves a mask into my hand—a white cat mask. Well, at least it goes with anything.

"Thanks, Ariella," Nerissa responds for us. The hostess flicks her light brown locks and simpers at us.

As we pull on our masks, Dorian grimaces at Nerissa, "You are so cliché."

"Am not! Not like you can talk with your matching set."

"That's not what I—"

"Hey," Douglas cuts in. "How about we get to our spot while there's still room to move in this joint?"

Inside is a sea of hidden faces, whooping it up to the latest remixed tracks. I try not to lose sight of my bestie in the horde of intoxicated dancers. We head toward the private room Nerissa has managed to reserve for us. As we finish crossing the floor, a slightly smaller man mountain opens the velvet rope to the main VIP room. He lets us in, and then gets on the two-way. We all settle on the plush semicircle lounges before our waitress comes to take our orders.

I beckon Nerissa to come closer. "How did you swing this?"

"I convinced Uncle Conway that this was what I wanted for my birthday."

"But your birthday is still three months away." I look at her incredulously.

"I know, but—"

Nerissa is cutoff by a dashing man in his early thirties—Uncle Conway. His hair may once have been blond like his young relatives, but it's now a mousy color that's rather non-descript. He surveys me with interest, taking my hand in his and bows lightly before kissing it. "So this is the Mishca I have heard so much about?"

Douglas stiffens. I groan inwardly. There's way too much testosterone in this little space.

"Nerissa, my pearl, drinks are on the house all night, but do not get me into trouble with your father. My sister may forgive her baby brother every time, but your father does not." Conway turns to me again. "What's your poison and I will deliver it personally?"

"Water," I reply shortly.

"I will arrange that for you." I give Nerissa death stares.

"Hey, what am I to do," she protests in her defense. "I can't help it if my friend and uncle both are interested in filling the void in your love life."

I shoot her a glare, proving yet again I don't have heat vision, but kind of wishing I did.

The first round of drinks comes: Black Sambuca shots, along with a bunch of cocktails for the girls, a mocktail for me, and beers for the guys. After all the glasses are empty, someone suggests hitting the dance floor. I take the opportunity to let go of all my frustrations and cut loose.

That prickling sensation ripples over my arms. *Crap, not tonight.* I'd been doing so well controlling my strength, hearing, and freakiness in general. I whip my head around and see Colin, dancing with a group. I think I recognize some of them as lecturers and staff from the university. Around his neck hangs a plain black mask. I stop dancing and slide my cat mask up to make sure I'm really seeing this.

As though he senses my stare, Colin turns and faces me. Like a scene from a cheesy romance, he moves toward me, oblivious to the questions from his friends, or to the people he strides past on his way to me. He doesn't pause when he reaches me, instead he grasps my face and kisses me gently.

The jolt that happened when we first touched is nothing compared to this kiss. Images of Colin laughing, kissing me, sweaty above me as he makes love to me, flash in my mind like fireworks.

Without a word, he leads me off the dance floor into a secluded spot. He turns me against the wall, pressing his body to mine. We both gasp, but continue locked together. He holds my shoulders firm with both hands as he kisses me deeper. One of his hands slides up and gently grips the back of my neck. I moan when Colin moves his mouth across my cheek in a series of light kisses, and then works his way to my neck. His teeth graze my skin in a playful nip before he sucks. The hand on my shoulder moves down and finds my breast, cupping it. Every touch is like déjà vu.

Sorrow washes over me for Ryder. I gulp. I don't understand how Colin is filling the emptiness inside with every kiss.

"We need to stop," I say, pushing Colin back. "I need to know what this is."

He nods. "I know."

"Let's sit down and talk." I grasp his hand and lead him to our private booth.

Once settled into our seats I decide to test Nerrisa's theory. "Someone you love didn't die late last year, did they?"

He looks at me like I've grown a second head. "No."

"Okay, that's a good start." *Stupid Nerissa.*

"Why did you ask that?" Colin's shoulders go ridged with tension.

"Oh, it's nothing. Just a friend speculating some stupid stuff." *My replacement heart doesn't love Colin, and I haven't been possessed by his dead ex's spirit.* "You don't have any theories, do you?"

"One. You remind me a lot of someone. I thought maybe it was me missing her, wanting a person to fill that void." He looks away.

The music consumes our conversation. I don't know where to go from here. "I'm adopted," I blurt out.

"Really?"

"You wouldn't sound so surprised about it if you had met my parents," I say. "There's no mistaking it. They're both white." Not wanting to go over old territory, I quickly shift gears. I need to see if there's something more here than this physical attraction. "So where'd you go to uni? Here in Brisbane?"

Colin shakes his head. "No, I actually went to America to study."

This time my eyebrows go up. That is a huge step in my books. A lot of kids from school went and backpacked in Europe, taking a gap year, but straight over to the United States to study? Wow.

"What made you do that?"

The longing on his face shows he's there again in his mind, recapturing his youthful exploits, but then the sadness returns.

"A girl. I followed a girl to America."

"Really? Was she the one who hurt you?" I can't help wanting to know more but recoil at my blatant snooping. "Sorry, I shouldn't pry."

"No, it's okay. It's about time I talked about it to someone, and it's appropriate it's you. Her name was Imogene, and she was my wife."

The silence hangs between us again. He has been married, and she left. Enough to hurt, yes, but this level of hurt—that must have been one painful breakup. I tap my fingernails against my glass of water.

"What was she like?" I can't help asking.

After hesitating, Colin succumbs. "She was a lot like you—vibrant, full of life—and she affected me instantly, as you did. You remind me so much of her. Immy was an exchange student at my school as part of a musical theater program, and the instant she walked into my homeroom I was smitten. We were inseparable all senior year, and when she returned to America to continue her studies, I followed a year later, proposed, and she said yes."

"But she left you? How could she leave you? You left everything for her!" *Whoa. Where did that come from?*

Colin's eyes dance with glistening moisture. "She didn't have a choice."

Before I can ask anymore, another round of drinks magically appears.

"Courtesy of Conway," says the waitress with a wink.

I guzzle down one of the drinks but always keep contact with Colin. He slides his arm around me. I fit perfectly beside him.

"Have I told you how beautiful you look tonight?" he whispers in my ear.

I shiver and turn my face to his. His eyes bore into mine. Our mouths inch together. His hand cups my chin, bringing my face close. Sparks fly off my lips when they touch his. His hand moves around the back of my neck. Our kisses are gentle at first then grow hungrier, his tongue pushing into my mouth and exploring. He pulls me onto his lap, like he's desperate to get as much body contact with me as possible.

I have no idea how long we kiss before finally coming up for air. He traces my jawline with his finger. I want to stay in his arms forever, but the drinks I've consumed have other ideas.

"I have to go to the ladies," I say, squirming from his embrace.

What the heck are you doing? My head spins like a defective Ferris wheel out of control. *What about Ryder?*

I love Ryder; I know that now. It's taken time away to see it, to know it. But if I could love him, and still be so attracted to Colin, I need to find out why. I use the facilities quickly, my mind whirring over the crazy situation I've put myself in. As I make my way back across the dance floor, hands slip around my hips from behind.

Colin! Instead of Colin's dress shoes, I see a pair of chunky boots. Turning around to slap my assailant, a feathery black mask framed in luscious green hair greets me.

"Hey, sugarplum." She plants one on my lips. "You taste good. What you been drinking, virgin sex on the beach?"

I grit my teeth at Sophitia's leering.

"Leave her alone, Tia."

Blue feathers and spikey black hair frame eyes that are normally blue but now flash purple. Sophitia turns to Ryder and smirks before slinking into the crowd.

"Sorry about that."

His voice slices through to my core. My lips tingle in anticipation of a kiss that isn't coming. *I miss you.* "That's okay. Not like it was your fault anyway. Um, when did you get here?"

His mouth remains tight. "Just now. Tia was on the list, so we didn't have to wait. Otherwise, we still wouldn't be in the door. How about you?"

I try my best to sound nonchalant. "A few hours ago." Calculations aren't even necessary. He wouldn't have seen Colin and me making out. *Thank goodness.* I look away, ashamed, glancing at the private booth. Colin must have been staring at me as we instantly make eye contact. *I'm such a dumbass.* Ryder's gaze follows mine.

"So that is the reason you needed space."

I nod on autopilot. "Kind of. But I didn't cheat on you." *Not physically.*

Shaking his head in bewilderment, Ryder stalks away without another word to join his group by the bar. I gasp for breath as though all the oxygen has been removed from the room. It takes so much to stop from running after Ryder. I want to. I miss him so much. I stare after him contemplating which voice I should listen to in my head. *Ryder or Colin.*

Along with Ryder and Sophitia, dance Steven and Perdi in matching masks. Two tall guys, one with blond hair in a ponytail and a silvery spider-web mask, and the other with longer, loose hair that frames a mask covered in twisted vines; and a girl with black hair and a blond fringe set atop a glimmering blue mask that reminds me of crystals all mill around. The guy with the vines is in deep conversation with Nixie, who giggles a lot with her hand coming to her mouth. The others start moving away, escaping to our private room. I retreat there too. Nixie follows me.

Everyone else is back at the booth and poor Colin looks the odd one out. Nerissa gives me a significant look and inclines her head at him, mouthing a, "what?" I manage a shrug.

Nerine raises her eyebrows. "Having fun, Nixie?"

A pointed tongue is the only answer. Moments later, a waitress comes over with a round of drinks. "Compliments of Coen." From the viney slimy who was talking to Nixie, I'm guessing.

I'm not going to be able to touch mine, so I pass it to Colin. Everyone sniffs, and then drinks deeply, resulting in a round of coughing and spluttering — with the exception of Colin.

"What is this stuff?" gasps Nerine.

"I don't know, but they were all drinking it fine," Nixie says, her voice rising in pitch.

"It's absinthe." All heads swivel to Colin who has finished his and moved onto mine. "And if I am not mistaken, this is the real stuff and not the replicates that meet Australian standards."

"So this is illegal?" asks Douglas. "Cool."

"Well, it was Van Gough's poison of choice, but then again, he cut off his ear, so I'm not sure how cool this stuff is to drink all the time. Occasionally, it's nice."

Ah, Obi Wan, you have taught them well. Colin lets a satisfied smirk settle across his face.

After polishing off my third water, I need to go powder my nose again. In true girl-power form, Nerissa follows.

"Are we cool?" I ask as we wash our hands.

"Yeah, baby doll. Who am I to judge? I only wish you'd warned me. Douglas had his hopes up."

"I had no idea he would be here." I raise my brows in the mirror.

She scrunches her nose. "Or that you'd be playing tonsil hockey with him."

I palm my face. "And Ryder saw him. Everything is so messed up. I can't explain why I have feelings for Colin."

Nerissa shoots a sideways glance at me. "So does that mean you have feelings for Ryder still?"

"Of course I do. It's just so...complicated."

Nerissa heads in front to clear a path, grabbing my hand at first, but our clammy palms slip as we enter the throng. A chill ripples over me, and then someone clutches my arm. That feeling is back, the tingling that starts at my toes and takes over my whole body. I've felt it at the chapel and whenever I see the not-so-nice reflection of me. *Crud, am I about to start hallucinating again?*

"Been sleeping well lately? I am sure your sleep is more enjoyable when you dream of me."

I turn in horror to see a man all in black with a plain red mask. His eyes are hidden in shadows, but his long brown hair and square stubble jaw aren't. He looks so familiar, but he scares me to my core. *Creepiest pick-up line ever.*

"Sorry, do I know you?"

He leers at me, making me shudder. "If not yet, it won't be long now. Find me in your dreams."

As loudly as I can I scream, "Hey, get your hands off me, jerk." Only people close by react. A cat-masked girl with an afro laughs while a man in a black suit, green tie, and matching green mask watches impassively.

A large man dressed in a long trench coat and plain black mask steps forward. "Are you bothering this young lady?"

The red-masked man drops his hand. "Not at all." Then, he evaporates into the crowd.

Hastily I retreat, but as I turn, I smack straight into someone's chest. Ryder has taken his mask off and stares down at me, brows pinched together. "Are you okay?"

"Yeah, I'm fine."

"Do you need an escort?"

"Colin's here so I—" I gesture to our room, and then let my arm drop. Ryder's face hardens, but before he can respond, hands slip around his waist, the thumbs wedging into the top of his pants.

"Ryder, where have you been? You left me waiting. I don't like to be kept waiting." The small girl with the blue crystal mask maintains her hold on her prey, twisting her body around Ryder's to gain eye contact.

"Sorry, Shona. I was distracted. Now I am *all* yours."

Even though I've no right to, jealousy gremlins scramble my stomach and an urgent desire to rip her face off rises. I stalk to our booth still stinging that Ryder has moved on already. My gaze falls on Colin. I drop my head. It's what I deserve.

"Hey, there you are."

"I'm done for the night, " I say, eager to avoid watching Ryder with another girl. I turn to Nerissa. "Will you be right to get home without me?"

She nods.

"I'll walk you out." Colin gets to his feet.

I shake my head. "I think I need some time alone."

His mouth drops, but he says, "I understand. I want to see you again. Is that okay?"

I hesitate, and then nod. Part of me wants to get to the bottom of what the deal is with Colin and me, but the other half wants to run to Ryder.

CHAPTER 26

"WHERE ARE WE GOING?" The anticipation is killing me. We've been driving for such a long time.

"We're almost there," says Colin, placing a hand on my leg.

Instead of picking me up in the Holden Statesman sedan I saw him with at uni, Colin picked me up in a ute — it looks like a cross between a coupe and a baby pickup truck. Mysterious bags are in the back that I'm not allowed to even take a peek at. Thankfully, Dad was out of town for a game again. Mum did insist on meeting Colin, but to her credit, she didn't make a fuss. She shot me a look that made it clear we would be discussing it later.

The excitement pulses over my body, making me feel like I'm going to explode. It has been so long since I've been this happy, so long since I was this content. *When was the last time I was this happy? It had to be…Ryder.*

I push the thought away. Maybe this will work. Maybe this is what's meant to be. This is my chance to find out if Colin and I belong together. I've stopped fighting these feelings, and my body likes that I've succumbed.

"Okay, you can take it off now."

Goodness knows what other people think when they see a man in his late thirties with a nineteen-year-old blindfolded in the passenger seat of his car. Luckily, it's dusk. My vision has a little readjusting to do as I slip off my scarf which Colin turned into a makeshift blindfold.

A drive-in! I've never been to one before in my life. There's less and less of them around nowadays.

"Oh, this is so cool."

Colin turns to me, grinning like a kid about to unwrap presents on Christmas morning. "Are you sure? I know that these places aren't 'hip' anymore." I suppress a snigger. *Who uses the word "hip"?* "But you wanted to know about what I did when I was younger. Well, this was a big part of it."

Purely content—that's me. Not only has Colin remembered, but he has delivered.

"So what are we going to see?"

"Well, there weren't a lot of options. But a friend of mine…" *Which friend? It'd better not have been a woman.* I try to focus on his words, but the jealousy is immediate and all consuming. *Where did that come from?* "... told me that *Independence Day* was best experienced at the drive-in."

"Ahh, yeah," I plaster a smile on and banish wayward thoughts, "classic Will Smith. I like it."

"Yeah, Richard said it was amazing to look up at. Well, wait and see."

I reach over and take Colin's hand. "It's great. This was definitely on my need-to-rewatch list."

Before us is a massive car park segmented with tiny poles showing allotted spots. Colin finds a nice one in the middle and drives in.

The ute, decked out with sleeping bags and pillows, is surprisingly comfortable. We settle in and watch the ads. Tonight's vintage night, but it doesn't stop them from flogging the latest and greatest upcoming movies. I can't help but wonder how many guys refuse to use the speaker hanging off the side of the vehicle because they worry about their paint job. I snuggle right in, inhaling every essence of Colin I can. He smells of spices and sandalwood. This feels so natural, like he's been with me all my life, and I haven't realized it until now.

Not long into the movie, clouds roll overhead on the screen as the alien ships emerge. My gaze shifts skyward, automatically scanning the clouds in case any mirror the ones I've seen on-screen. They illuminate in the moonlight, looking too much like the movie for my liking. But then again, I have an overly active imagination.

"Enjoying it?" Colin whispers. I turn to him and nod. He's so close his breath tickles my skin. Neither of us look at the screen again until the end credits. From the audio, I'm guessing Will Smith kicked some alien butt, and the United States prevailed to save the human race. It doesn't bother me as I've already seen it. All I want is for it to hurry up and end so we can be alone.

* * * *

The whole room seems to be on fire, and my skin tingles as the temperature rises in Colin's apartment. A strangled noise comes out of his throat before he catches his breath. "Oh, Mishca. I... it's been so long, and I don't want to dis—"

I bring my fingers to his lips which he instinctively begins to kiss. "It's okay. I haven't...you know...before."

"Oh? Oh! Are you sure then? I wouldn't want to rush you."

I bite my lip and nod nervously. "I'm sure." *Not really.* My heart says yes, but my head says, *Are you crazy girl?*

Every move he makes shows his experience and my lack of it. Then, everything comes to an abrupt halt.

No, not again.

"Mishca, not like this." He gently takes my hand. "Your first time should be perfect."

"It will be. Don't stop."

It's Colin's turn to silence me with his fingers. "Follow me."

I walk hand-in-hand with Colin down the hall. We come to a room at the end. Inside is a massive bed. He scoops me into his arms, carries me over the threshold, and lays me on the blue quilt cover.

The biggest smile of my life spreads across my face. "Come here you."

Together we peel off my jacket. A look of pure adoration greets me before his gaze shifts to the next piece of clothing to be removed. Warm hands creep under my shirt, pulling it up over my head.

I want to grab his hand and yank it away. Horror overwhelms me. I've forgotten to fill Colin in on my medical history. Everything has moved so fast, there hasn't been time. Well, that's what I'm telling myself. Adoration is replaced with shock.

A hoarse whisper escapes Colin's lips, "What is that?"

"I'm sorry. I should have told you, but I never found the right time. Short version is I had a heart defect, and last year, I had a heart transplant. But don't worry, the recovery manual says I'm fine to have sex."

But it isn't right. Something's wrong...very wrong. Colin's face has not changed. There's no acknowledgement of what has been said. Not even a, "you should have told me," not anything until he cracks. "I can't do this. Not again. I can't…I have to go. Don't be here when I get back."

Then, he's gone. I'm left half undressed in a strange bed where I'm no longer welcome. I close my eyes and listen intently, following his footsteps as he races out of the apartment, down the stairs, and out the door. He's lost to me, and I'm left alone.

CHAPTER 27

"MISHCA, ARE YOU SURE you want to do this?"

I nod. Nerissa and I look ridiculous. We're meant to be breaking in to Colin's place, so I said to dress in black. But obviously, we don't own a lot of house-breaking attire. Shimmery leggings and lacy tops with sequins hardly make us blend into the shadows.

Through the gloom I spot a figure leaning against the building. I use standardized signals for close-range engagement to alert Nerissa — clench fist (freeze), index finger up (one), clasp my index finger and thumb around my forearm (enemy).

"Huh?"

I frown in frustration. It's basic CRE 101 stuff. *Wait, how did I know the acronym for close range engagement? Or what it meant? Or how to do it?*

"Somebody's there!" I whisper fiercely. My counterpart in crime gulps and peeps around the corner before sighing with relief. "It's Ryder!"

"Ryder!" I hiss. "Did you have him come here to try and stop me?"

"No, he was the only person I knew who could pick a lock," the traitor's sheepish response.

Seeing Ryder sends off fireworks inside. And promptly confuses the heck out of me. *I almost had sex with Colin! How can I flip flop so much? What is wrong with me?* But warmth settles across my heart that can't be denied at Ryder's approach.

His face is stone until we get close enough for him to see our getups. "Hello, ladies. How are tricks?"

Instinctively, I punch him in the arm. Ryder, of course, has on a black Nike tracksuit and appears casually wonderful.

I turn to Nerissa. "Would you go double check that we locked the car doors?"

"Um yeah, sure," she replies, knowing full well we did.

I wait until she's by the car. My face burns red, but now that I've got Ryder alone I babble, "Do you know that Sophitia likes girls?"

Ryder bursts out laughing. "Did she make a move on you?"

"Uh-huh."

"Sorry, I should have warned you. Yes, Sophitia swings both ways."

He laughs harder as my blush deepens.

"Very funny." I now regret bringing it up. "I thought she liked you. The two of you always seemed like a good match. You both avoid contractions when you speak and—"

"No, I do not." Ryder clamps his hand over his mouth. "Sophitia is like a sister to me. Nothing more."

I contemplate telling him that she's not his sister, and in fact is his cousin, but then Nerissa heads back over. I sigh and decide to change the subject. "Could we please get this over with?"

The stone face returns. No retort to my grammar error sends anxiety clawing at my stomach. He says nothing as he jimmies the apartment complex's front door until there is a *pop* and a *click*. A few minutes later, we repeat the process at Colin's apartment.

Ryder assumes the position at the front door to play lookout while Nerissa and I wonder where to start.

"What are we even trying to find?" Nerissa asks.

"I don't know. But there has to be something to explain why he bailed on me."

"Oh, yeah, because it has to be him, not you that's the problem." Ryder's harsh tone guts me.

I let it slide. He has a right to be angry with me. I still have feelings for Ryder. He was my first real boyfriend and will always have a special place in my heart. How can I explain to him that I simultaneously love Colin, and I felt that love at first-sight? Who does that?

"How about we split up and take a room each?" says Nerissa.

It's a good plan. The apartment isn't big. It has a combined dining and living room, a master bedroom, a spare room used as a study, a bathroom, and a kitchen. The latter two are priorities for the search.

"Okay, then I'll take the bedroom," I say, causing a shadow to pass over Ryder's face. "Nerissa, you take the study, and Ryder, you check the living room, but still keep an eye on the door."

I start down the hall, but a warm hand on my arm stops me in my tracks.

"He didn't *hurt* you, did he, Mishca?" The hushed tone reflects the concern etched on Ryder's face.

I shake my head. "No, not like that...we didn't...I can't talk about this with you. I just need answers."

Reluctantly, he releases me to begin my search.

We've been carefully prowling through Colin's things for half an hour when the silent searching is interrupted.

"What. The. Fuck!"

Ryder shouts from the living room. I hurry, relieved as I am to come across anything useful. With Nerissa in tow, we traverse the hallway and see Ryder whipping something in his hand behind him.

"What? What is it?"

"Nothing. False alarm."

"Come on, Ryder, please don't torment me like this."

He won't look me in the eye and speaks to Nerissa as though I'm not even there. "Nerissa, please get her out of here. She needs to let this go. Trust me." Then, he finally turns to me. "Forget about him. I am not saying this because I still love you. For your own good, you need to forget you ever met him. Move on. I do not even care if it is with me or not. This is too important. Never try to see him again."

Goldfish look more intelligent than me right now. Firstly, what is so bad that Ryder refuses to let me see, and secondly…he *still* loves me?

Taking advantage of my dumbfounded state, Nerissa swoops in. "Here, let me see. It can't be that bad." Catching Ryder off-guard, she snatches the contents out of his hands: a small leather-bound book with something jutting out. *A piece of paper? No, a photo.* As she opens the book to the page with the photo, her expression changes like seasons across her face: confusion at first then angst, then anger, and finally, sadness as she turns the photo over and reads the back.

"No," she says in such a soft whisper it sends a chill down my spine. *If Nerissa thinks it is bad…*"Listen to him. Let's go. Now."

I can't. I can't move at all. Our standoff continues until it is interrupted by the jangling of keys in a lock.

"Oh. Fuck." The delightful language comes from Ryder again. I take the opportunity to lunge forward for the bounty. Quickly, Nerissa steps back, but the photo is dislodged from its resting place and floats to the floor. The words *Imogene and Colin: Wedding Day* written in black ink capture my attention. Determined, I reach for the photo as the door opens.

"What's going on here?"

I turn to face my love, photo in hand. I glance down at the image I'm holding, gazing between the Colin of today and a younger version of him in the wedding photo. Standing beside the younger Colin is me. Well, not me, but the woman staring back at me with a gloating smirk, like the cat who got the cream, is a mirror image: the eyes, the nose, the lips. Some differences show, but only slight. The lack of a scar—the wedding dress has a plunging neckline—and the hair could very well be how mine would turn out if I ever went to a salon and got it straightened. She looks older, more mature, but not by much. *We could pass for…* The urge to crunch up the photo and throw it in *his* face is overwhelming. *How could he?*

"Care to explain?" I spit the words like sewage in my mouth. When I hold the photo to my face, Imogene and I are cheek to cheek.

"Explain what? I told you that you reminded me of her."

An explosion erupts inside me. "Did you ever consider, for even a moment, particularly after I spoke about being adopted, that you could be dating your daughter?" The age was right. So much fit. A paternal bond would explain the love I feel. *But it's not that type of love.*

"No! No!" The denials continue. "No, you can't be. I never…We never had the chance to have children. I can't even have children. I'm sterile."

Nerissa interrupts, "But they are so much alike. Is there any chance that she had a child?"

Colin protests, "No! She waited for me. There's no way."

"But you were apart for a year. Mishca told me so," Nerissa presses.

Colin's face falters. There appears to be some truth resonating that he hasn't considered before.

"Dude." Ryder can't seem to help himself. "I think you have been dating your stepdaughter."

"Where is she, Colin? I need to know. She could be my mother."

Colin takes a step away and shifts so I can no longer see his face. "You can't see her, Mishca."

"Oh come off it. Stop jerking her around." The air around Ryder rises in temperature, stifling the room.

"You can't see her," Colin repeats, facing me again, cheeks damp with tear streaks, "because she's dead."

"You said she left, and it wasn't her fault." An eerie calm washes over me. "How did she die?"

"Her heart. She was born with a heart defect. It was after we got married. They found a donor, and she had the operation. But it didn't work. Her body rejected it. There was nothing they could do to save her."

Silence settles over us until I determine what I have to do. "Come on. Let's go." I don't look back.

CHAPTER 28

"IF THAT IS WHAT you want to do, okay. But we might need backup. My house is on the way." Ryder breaks the long silence that follows the outlining of my plan.

"If he's up for it."

None of us speak again until we arrive at Ryder's. Almost aimlessly, I follow him into the house. My thoughts drift to Colin, and my anger renews full blast, but the love lingers, as much as I wish it would disappear. *Why do I look so much like her? Is that why I feel this way about Colin? How is any of this real?* Ryder bangs on Finlay's door. A beautiful young woman wrapped in nothing but a sheet opens the door a crack. Annoyed and hair tousled, she easily passes for Medusa's better-looking sister.

"Is he in?"

Groggy and in boxers, Finlay appears and leans his arm against the doorframe, bicep bulging. He glances at his friend, and then scowls when he sees me.

"I need your help."

Some guy code kicks in, and although not another word is spoken between the two friends, within five minutes we're on to the next stop.

This time Ryder knocks politely instead of nearly bashing down the door. An alert Connor emerges. "Hey. What's up?"

"We need your expertise," Ryder says, and again the guy code sees us inside the apartment. As Connor picks up his laptop, the screen flashes toward us, revealing Perdi's Facebook profile.

"Man," exclaims Finlay. "You're not cyber stalking, are you?"

Even in the dark Connor's pale face flashes crimson.

I've waited long enough. "I need an address for *EEFS*."

It takes Connor a moment to process. "Tried the white pages?"

Ryder interjects, "You know the deal with *them*. We need a location, and we need it *now*."

Fingers flurry over the keyboard. It's not long before Connor gives a triumphant cry, "Got it!"

"You have an address?" I whoop ecstatically.

"Nope. I couldn't crack into their full system, but I entered their public site through the back door. It won't be long now."

True to his word, in minutes, Connor passes me a piece of paper with a Brisbane address for Eleithyia Elite Family Services. He grabs a small messenger bag and slings it over his shoulder.

"Doubt they have filing cabinets waiting for you to rifle through. I'm pretty sure I will be able to access their system fully for you given a bit more time. On site might help."

Finlay shrugs at Ryder, and then we all head out.

* * * *

I'm continually scanning the area to identify threats and the best possible escape route. It's a shame we don't have access to a helicopter as the roof is optimal for an emergency exit. I slip into standardized signals for close range engagement. This soldier stuff has become so second nature to me now that I forget to be frightened by it. The theory Dr. Thompson experimented on me is looking a more and more likely scenario.

Finlay and Connor emerge from the shadows, dressed in dark clothes as well. I didn't hear anyone, or see any lights on, so hopefully no back-up is required.

"This better be worth it," grumbles Fin. "I left some sweet arse at home for this."

Ryder glowers, silencing him, and stopping Connor from making a peep. A large brick building with wooden barricaded windows looms before us. We move together in a pack toward the front door. I hold my breath as Ryder works on the lock.

"I can't get it," he says after a few minutes.

Hello, super-strength ex-girlfriend here.

"Here, let me give it a try."

My hand clenches the handle, and I push down with all my might. It groans and creaks under the pressure. There's a snap, but the door's still locked. I center my energy and put my shoulder into the door. The wooden frame cracks. I shoot everyone a triumphant fist pump before Finlay motions us inside.

A sparse waiting area greets us at the front with another access point on the other side of the room. No muscle skills needed this time. It opens onto a corridor with five doors, two on either side and one at the end. The first three we open are for storage, two filled with what seem to be chemicals and a third with food. The last one on the left is stocked with filing cabinets. I can't help but shoot Connor a smirk. Without hesitating, we all start sliding drawers open and rifling through. I find a file marked *Donors*, but there's nothing about me.

"Eureka!" Nerissa calls, holding up a file labeled Mishca Richardson. She thumbs through the contents which includes recent photos. *Creepy*. A shudder runs through me. Connor stuffs the file into his bag. Obviously, it's got way too much in it to sort on the spot. The five of us spill into the hallway to be greeted by angry voices from the lobby—security. I slip back into issuing orders with CRE standardized signals.

"Mishca, stop fooling around," says Finlay, grabbing my hands and lowering them. "As accurate as those are, I'm pretty sure I'm the only one here who gets them."

My eyebrows head for my hairline, but I say nothing.

"Quick, this way." Ryder drags me toward the door at the rear. My skin begins to tingle as we enter the new area. It's like I've got static electricity all over my body, and an energy tugs me to the center of the room. In contrast to the dingy hallway, everything here is clean and glossy black. Down to the right are rows of tall shelves with boxes. Shiny surfaces glisten in the light of a huge monitor that would rival a cinema screen sitting atop a curved desk. It flickers to life, and then everything goes black.

Electricity shimmers in the room. I can't see anything, but it prickles my skin. When my vision clears, I focus on the monitor.

"Subject AMR detected." A new voice, smooth, monotone, and female, echoes through the room. In my peripheral vision I see my friends spin around, searching for the voice. But I remain still.

A holographic keyboard hangs over the desk, prompting Connor to rush over, USB stick in hand.

"Interfacing," the voice continues, "Scanning. Defects detected. Non-life-threatening. Repairs initiated."

A small red laser beam, originating from the top of the computer, hits my chest, spreading warmth throughout my body. I go rigid, unable to move. The others don't seem to notice.

"We need to buy ourselves some time," says Ryder.

"Give me a hand," replies Fin.

To my right, the two of them struggle with a large cabinet in an attempt to barricade the door. Grunting and groaning, they manage to edge the large cabinet over the entrance. In front of me, Connor searches around like a man possessed. When his eyebrows shoot up in triumph, he inserts his USB stick into a computer tower underneath the desk and reaches toward the holographic screen. A soft light emanates from my skin.

The angry voices grow louder. The guards must be closer. Someone swears, though I'm not sure who. My body tenses at the imminent threat but remains still.

"Mishca!" Nerissa shrieks shrilly. "Wake up. Snap out of it. We have to go."

"This is off the hook!" Connor exclaims.

Files, images, and words flash across the large monitor as his hands race in midair. He pauses on the files, "Alpha Female" and "Alpha Male." The first file opens to reveal a picture of a woman who looks so much like me, just older. Across the image in big red letters are the words *Subject Deceased*. With a flick of his wrist, Connor opens the second file to reveal a photo of a stocky young man with such a short haircut it could only have been army issued. The same wording is stamped across the picture. The name underneath reads Adam Manning, and the scarlet words, *Subject Terminated*.

"Dude, is that your dad?" says Ryder.

Connor taps on the file, "Female Subjects." Still frozen in place, I begin to read.

Base subject found to be inferior after duplication process began. Of the fifty initial subjects created, only four have survived. Subject AMR exhibited signs of defect but has been temporarily repaired by external sources. Subject APJ's degeneration has not reached critical stage and intervention by operative Wirth was successful. Intervention attempted with subject AMC, but repairs were not viable. Subject AMC to be destroyed. Subject ATK's and AAR's statuses are unknown. Termination recommended.

The female voice rings out again, "Physical-deficiency repairs complete. Rebooting subject's internal hardware."

A blue laser beam slices through the air into my eyes. The computer image displays the repairs to my heart.

To my right, Ryder dashes forward, tackling me to the ground. I go from rigid to floppy like a ragdoll. My body won't move no matter how hard I try. Ryder covers me protectively. I want to crack a joke but can't manage to croak more than incoherent words. Banging and shouting starts on the other side of the door.

"Connor, we need to move," cries Finlay.

Nerissa whimpers in the corner. Fin scoops her into his arms without speaking.

"I've got it all," says Connor, guiding the USB stick free and tucking it into his pocket.

Ryder awkwardly struggles to his knees before jerking into a standing position. I flop around in his arms, perfectly still. Although I'm not heavy, it will be a struggle to get us all out before the people on the other side of the door catch up. The cabinet has already begun to give against the constant pressure.

Move, your squad is in danger. My body reconnects with my mind, and I struggle free of Ryder's arms. I scan the room for an exit point. *There.* On the far side of the shelves is a door. I run to it, but it opens before I get to it.

A huge man in a long black coat steps forward. I shift into combat stance. Nerissa shrieks.

"Do not be alarmed. I am here to help you. It was foolish to come here. No matter now."

I do a double take at the translucent grey color of his skin and his amber eyes. Although he is a stranger, he looks familiar. He's close to seven feet tall and has shoulders as broad as Ryder's and Finlay's put together. I think I can take him if I need to. I'm sure of it. His hard-set jaw and scowl make me uneasy, but there's no time to argue as a final crack at the door sends the cabinet toppling over and four security guards tumble in.

They stand and hesitate for a second, taking in the scene. The man in the black coat winks at me.

"Let us go forth into the fray!"

He lets loose a bellow that sounds exactly as I have always imagined a battle cry, but it ends in a roar so primitive it's almost animalistic. I follow after him, ignoring the protests of my squad, and after a flurry of kicks and punches, our enemies lie still on the floor, not terminated. Their chests move with their breaths.

"Well, that was hardly worth the roar," the stranger says, standing over them. "'Tis not to be helped now, though. Follow, young ones, there is a way out through here."

The beast of a man strides to the entrance and beckons us to follow. A strange amount of bulk bulges under his coat, particularly at his back, and I wonder if he's on steroids.

I follow him with Ryder in tow. Next come Connor and Finlay, still carrying Nerissa. We enter the room and find brightly glowing fluorescents and a gurgling noise. My eyes strain to readjust to the new lighting levels, and as they do bile rises in my throat.

"This is jacked up," mutters Finlay.

Connor loses his dinner almost immediately while the rest of us struggle not to retch. Each side of the room is filled with giant glass tubes that contain small fleshy blobs. The stench is horrendous.

"We must keep moving," hisses the stranger. "Those buffoons are not the real guardians of this place. It is only a matter of time before they are alerted."

As we edge our way along silently, I can't help but stare at the things inside the glass casings. They become less grotesque the further we go along until they look—

"Mishca, are you okay?" asks Ryder.

"Affirmative," I say.

"But—" The words stop when he peers at the final few rows of tubes. Inside people float. Most are adults, but to the left are babies.

"Through here," commands the giant, and we continue our way into a stairwell, proceeding upward.

Fin catches my attention and signals with his hands. *You. Me. Enemy.* He gestures to the stranger, and then continues. *Are you ready? Two. Commence fire.* I shake my head at the makeshift conversation. This guy is dangerous. There is no way I want to get on his bad side. At the moment, he considers us friends. I want it to stay that way. Connor moves like a zombie, but Nerissa is walking on her own now.

"What gives?" says Fin as we reach the empty rooftop. "I thought you must have a helicopter."

The grey-faced man shakes his head sorrowfully. "I am sorry for what I must now do."

Confused, I turn to confront him and am greeted by a clenched fist. I flinch and try to dodge, but it clips me. It's enough. I crumple. The last thing I remember is the thumping sound my head makes as it connects with the cement.

* * * *

Groggily I come to, finding myself on the pool deck at home. I try to shake away the fog but can't. I perch on the side of a sun chair. *How did I get here?*

"Mishca! Thank goodness you are all right." Ryder sits up slowly on one of the chairs. I'm relieved to see him and stumble over, checking him for any sign of injury. Smelly Belly rubs against his leg, purring.

He grabs my arms to stop my physical inspections. "We are safe now."

How can he know that for sure? I have no idea how we got here. *The best option is a perimeter check.* I straighten up too quickly, and my head starts to hurt. My hand searches around and finds a lump under my hair.

"What happened?" I ask. My memories stay trapped behind a fog. "I remember going to the EEFS building, and then it's a blur. I remember dreaming."

"You dreamed?"

I nod, chewing on my lip. "For once it wasn't all bad. It was vague, more like sensations and feelings. I recall being scared, prickling cascades through my body, and then blackness. I felt like I was being swallowed up whole. Things came clear for a bit. There were glass cylinders with people in them, and then it was black again. Suddenly, from nowhere, there was light. I was flying. The wind was on my face, in my hair. Next, I was here with you."

Ryder takes a deep breath, reaching for my hand, before explaining the events leading up to my blackout. But he abruptly stops talking and won't make eye contact. A chill goes through my body. *What's so bad that he won't talk about it?*

"And then what?" I prompt.

Ryder hesitates, glancing at me. "It does not matter. Connor downloaded some stuff. We can go through it with him later, and then we will have all the information. Some strange dude turned up out of nowhere and helped us escape. All that matters is that you are safe. But," he pauses, "the others, they — " he chokes on his words.

We're back to no eye contact. A ball of fear tightens in my stomach. The silence frustrates me, but I can't find any words. Before I can form a coherent thought, Ryder's phone beeps with an incoming message. He pulls his hands from mine to read it.

"Yes!" He hugs me, and then holds the phone to me so I can read the message. *Nerissa and Connor are with me. Are you okay? That freak knocked us out. But we've still got the USB stick. Call me when you can.*

"At least we got something from that lab," Ryder says.

I slink away from him, return to my chair, put my head in my hands, and lose myself in thought. *What lab?* A rush of scenes flash through my mind: a large black room, giant tubes with people floating in them, a weird screen, and a word that I now know applies to me. A word that I'm guessing Ryder can't bring himself to say.

I begin shaking all over. Tears spill down my cheeks and drip onto my legs. Ryder's face shows he understands I've acknowledged the truth. "I remember it all. I know who I am now. I have no parents." Something inside me shifts, breaks like a mirror into a thousand pieces. "I'm a clone."

CHAPTER 29

GLOWING GREEN LIQUID surrounds me. I bang against the glass. The water muffles my screams, gushing into my lungs. My chest burns.

"How can I love you?" Colin's voice comes booming across the dark room.

"How can anyone love you?" Ryder says, stepping into view. "A freak. Not even a real person."

"A cheap copy. An imitation." Colin appears before me.

"Who would want you?" asks a man with long brown hair.

He thrusts a blade through Colin. I scream again, my heart on fire. He wrenches the bloody blade out and slices it across Ryder's throat. My two loves slump to the ground in a heap.

"Only me. I'm the only one who wants you."

I gasp for air. Smelly Belly curls beside me, undisturbed. The dreams have been getting shorter.

Maybe I'm starting to master them. Or maybe I don't care anymore.

My phone beeps with an incoming message. I pick it up and see a ton of messages from Ryder and Nerissa. I ignore them and click on the Facebook app with the intention of deleting my account. A message in my inbox makes me pause. I wish I hadn't opened it immediately after I do. Another person mistaking me for Michelle Cooper. Now I understand why I've been mistaken for her. The phone slips from my hand. I continue to inspect the ceiling.

"Mishca," Mum hovers in my doorway, "will you be joining us for breakfast this morning?"

I can't find the strength to move. Despite the edge of concern in my mum's voice, I keep staring straight ahead. I've been in a fog of nightmares, both asleep and awake. The reality is worse than dreams. I'm even more an abomination than a freak. I'm not even a real human. I'm a fake, a fraud who stole someone else's face. And my love for Colin wasn't even real. It was her. Someone else. I've lost Ryder, who could have loved me. But not now — who would want me now?

"Is she coming down?" I hear Dad whisper followed by the sound of retreating footsteps. I focus my super hearing and keep listening to their conversation.

"No." Mum sounds like she's choking. "Do you think we should ask Dr. Thompson to make a house call?"

"I'm not sure if he's the right doctor for this. Maybe we should be contacting Dr. Usher?" Dad says. Mum's psychologist is the last person I want to speak to right now. "Alicia, it's been a week and we still don't have a clue why she won't get out of bed."

Has it been a week? I force my mind from the fog that has consumed me since our little breaking-and-entering excursion.

"But Tom, I'm not sure if she's been taking her medication. What if her body rejects the new heart? We could lose her."

"She has been. I've been checking. Let's give her a bit more time. If she doesn't snap out of it soon, then we'll call someone." Dad's tone becomes harsh. "Something must have gone on with her and Ryder, even though he denies it."

"But he looked so concerned. He wouldn't show his face if he'd done something wrong."

Their voices get fainter. For the first time in a week my heart flutters. Ryder had come around. I pick my phone up and go through the messages. They all say similar things. *I miss you. Call me. Are you okay?* I don't get how they could still want to have anything to do with a freak like me. *Freak.* The word bounces around in my head, and my heart hurts.

As safe as I feel hiding away from the world, the last thing I want is to see a doctor or a shrink. That's enough motivation to drag my sorry arse out of bed.

I stare in the mirror. *Ugh.* I see someone else's face, someone else's eyes, and someone else's lips. Nothing is mine. And my heart belongs to a different person again. My mind drifts to the woman I was created from—what did they call it? The base subject? *What was she like? Did she know about me?* There'll be no knocking on her door for a "surprise, I'm your daughter" reunion. *Is there a relationship term for a clone and their original?* I sink onto my bed, clutching my head.

Get up, Mishca. No more doctors. Not now. I grit my teeth and head to the bathroom for a much-needed wash. The transplant rules can go get stuffed. I'm having the hottest shower I can stand. The water pounds into my back and streams through my hair. My body sags with relief.

After soaking up the heat, I grab the strawberry-scented gel. Loofah in hand, I scrub as hard as I can. Nothing will get me clean enough. My skin has cherry red tinges. I give in to my body's protests and turn off the taps.

The thought of hanging around at home and facing a barrage of questions from Mum and Dad isn't appealing, so I get dressed. My body clock is all out of whack from sleeping so much. It's lunchtime. I don't take much care with my outfit, clutching the first dress my hand finds and some ballet flats.

I grab my keys, phone, and purse, and race for the garage.

"Going out for a drive. See you in a few hours," I call to Mum and Dad as I dash through the living room. I catch them off guard and manage to get to the garage without any questions. But not out of the garage.

"Mishca, wait," Dad calls from the doorway.

"I need some air. I'll be home in a few hours." I flash him the first smile that's graced my face for the past week. It's a fake one.

"We'll talk when you get back," he yells as I drive away.

A pang of pain constricts my chest. I watch our security gates close behind me. There's no way my parents will settle for zero explanation. *What if they kick me out once I tell them the truth? Can I tell them the truth? Am I even human? Why would they want me now?*

I drive aimlessly for about thirty minutes. The streets all look like carbon copies of each other. Clones.

Why me? I should just end this. I guide Betsy into a car park and release everything I've been holding in for the past week. My breath turns to ragged gasps. My body tenses as my rage mounts. Fists form and I strike out, letting free a primal yell. People walking nearby quicken their pace. *Breathe, Mishca.* Betsy's steering wheel buckles from my outburst. I do my best to mold it back into place. It's a stark reminder of the things that have manifested since my operation. Faster, stronger — a cloned atrocity.

The eruption of emotion subsiding, I decide to get out and walk around. The footpath is broken and uneven beneath my feet. Everything seems familiar, but my bearings haven't set in. I cross the road and spot the Bowl nightclub in front of me, quiet and silent in the afternoon sun. Normally, I'm here at night when it's bustling with nightlife. This is where I had my first kiss with Ryder, when I was just a freak and not an abomination, when life was good. My mouth goes dry thinking of Ryder. If only he were here to hold me. *I ruined a real thing with Ryder trying to work out a fake thing with Colin. I'm such a loser.*

It's too painful, so I continue on. A church a couple of blocks up comes into view. I have a bone to pick with God. Fists clenched, I march forward. The ancient building has grotesque gargoyles sitting on ledges that skirt the building's roof. The one above the doorway has almost human features, but it's too harsh, brutish. A vision of the cloning lab flashes before me of the man with grey skin — it looks like him. And so does the one at the hospital. My stomach turns, and I swallow bile.

I storm inside, past a nativity scene, my anger rising.

"Why would you do this to me?" I yell at the cross. "Why would you allow me to exist? Why didn't you stop them?"

My shoulders lighten. I slump into the pew. A haze settles over me. I let the fog take control of my senses. It's quiet. I sit there for so long that sleep pulls at me.

"Do you need to pray or talk?" My body jolts. The voice belongs to a young man whose green eyes and messy hair I've seen before, but I can't place him. I didn't even hear him sit down beside me.

"Praying and talking won't do me any good. I'm damned." I spit out the words.

"No one is damned. There is always hope for salvation." His voice is warm and gentle. Sincerity laces every word. But it does little to melt the ice around my heart.

"I don't even know if I have a soul to save." *A black hole of nothingness might be waiting for me when I die.*

"What makes you say that?" He leans forward.

"You wouldn't believe me." I fold my arms as if the motion will stop everything from spilling out.

"Try me."

I bite my lip and take a deep breath. "Heaven is for humans. Not abominations like me."

"You look human, you sound human. What else could you be?" He pauses, an internal light making his eyes sparkle. "Are you an alien?"

"No."

"Hath not a Jew eyes? Hath not a Jew hands, organs, dimensions, senses, affections, passions; fed with the same food, hurt with the same weapons, subject to the same diseases, healed by the same means, warmed and cooled by the same winter and summer, as a Christian is? If you prick us, do we not bleed? If you tickle us, do we not laugh? If you poison us, do we not die?"

"Ha. Ha." All the priests around and I have to pick the Shakespeare fanatic.

"I can't help you if you don't tell me." He places a hot and clammy hand on my arm.

I turn to him. "All right, what if I told you that I wasn't born, that I was created?"

"I would say God created us all."

"I don't know who created me, but it wasn't God."

"I beg to differ—"

"I came from a test tube!" I yell, getting to my feet.

"You're an IVF baby? Some churches frown on that, but it doesn't mean God doesn't love you," he counters, standing.

"No, you idiot!" I scream into his face. "I'm a clone!"

We both sink into the pew in silence. I bury my head in my hands.

When I finally finish he asks, "Do you think God didn't love Dolly?"

Dolly? What is this guy talking about? Then, I remember from science class: Dolly, the first animal ever cloned—a sheep.

"We cannot begin to fathom God's plan or the depth of his love. I've often mused that despite what some think about science disproving God, that our Father is actually the ultimate scientist who already knew all the secrets. He created life, after all. He knew how to make bodies and beings of all shapes and sizes that could sustain life, reproduce, and achieve great feats. Never doubt that your Father loves you, whether you were born of womb or test tube. God still implanted a soul in you with the spark of life, and He will love you for all eternity."

"I would so like to hurt you right now. And I could, easily. I'm dangerous." I want to reject what he's saying, but it resonates inside me. His words take the edge off my anger, but I still feel betrayed by God.

"Wait here." He hops up and walks into the sacristy. He's not much taller than me. I hope I didn't spit on him when I yelled.

The young man returns with a package, which he hands to me. Inside rests a Bible, a business card, and a cross on a necklace. I almost gasp at the beauty of the cross. It's intricately embossed gold with a large red stone set in the middle.

"I couldn't possible accept this." I try to pass it back to him.

"Nonsense. Put the cross on."

With trembling fingers, I pry open the clasp and secure it around my neck. The metal cools my chest where it touches flesh.

"Now remember, if ever things seem hopeless, look at the cross and know help is coming." He waves and walks away.

"Thank you," I call, dumbfounded.

"You're welcome, Mishca," he says and continues into the back room.

I take a minute to collect myself. A thought hits me, and an icy cold chill trickles down my body.

"Wait!" I yell, running to the closed door. I yank at the handle and throw open the door, but there's no one inside. My voice becomes a whisper. "I never told you my name."

I grab the business card from the box. His name is Markus.

CHAPTER 30

THE DRIVE HOME GIVES me a chance to figure out what I'm going to say to my parents. I have an epiphany behind the buckled steering wheel — and I'm totally amazed the car's still drivable. I manage to sneak upstairs and stash the package from Markus before going to find them.

How can I tell them the truth? I'd be out the door and locked up for research. At least the story I'm about to tell is close to the truth. Isn't that the best way to tell a lie? They sit across from me, their faces wrought with concern.

"I found my birth parents," I say.

Mum gasps and grabs Dad's hand. Her huge eyes tear up. She could pass for a manga character.

"I didn't know you were looking," Dad manages to say. His spare hand is gripping the armrest on his chair. His knuckles go white. "Why would that upset you so much? Did they hurt you?"

I shake my head. "No, I didn't meet them. I found them, and they weren't what I was expecting. You wouldn't be happy with them at all. I thought you wouldn't want me anymore." There is truth in my words and my tears.

My parents are on me in a flash, dragging me to my feet, arms squeezing me so tight I actually let out a squeak. Mum showers my face with kisses.

"Mishca," she says, finally giving my cheeks a rest. "We don't care where you came from. You're ours and you always will be."

I let my gaze drop to the floor. "Mum, if you knew the truth—"

"It wouldn't make any difference to how much we love you," Dad interjects.

His reassurance does little to settle my stomach. I want to throw up. They let go and give me some space to breathe. Smelly Belly enters the room and plops herself in front of Dad's chair.

"I think I'll go to my room for a bit."

"Sure thing, sweetheart," Dad says as he absentmindedly rubs the cat's stomach with his foot.

The creases on Mum's forehead smooth. I hate deceiving them. *It's only a variation of the truth.* I almost convince myself.

I trudge up the stairs to my self-imposed prison. *What do I do from here?* Christmas is a few months away still, but the deadline to reapply for uni is right around the corner. How do I push this aside and pretend I'm normal?

Sinking onto my bed, I stare at the ceiling. Part of me wants to go for a swim in our pool, but another part wants to keep interaction with real people to a minimum. My room is safe.

Mum clearing her voice from the doorway interrupts my zone-out.

"Mishca, honey. Ryder's here. Do you want to see him?"

"Sure, Mum. Would you mind if I see him in here?" No way I want to risk them overhearing anything Ryder has to say.

"Not a problem. I'll send him up." They must still be worried if they're letting me around the no-boys-in-the-room policy.

I sit on my bed, waiting. A timid tapping on the door is followed by an apprehensive face.

"How are you doing?" For once there's no cheeky smile.

"Been better. You?"

"Trying to come to terms with it all. I am sorry, Mishca. I can only imagine what it has been like for you this last week." He stands at the door, hands jammed in his jeans' pockets.

"Hey, no, it's okay."

"So what do you make of it all?" Ryder stares at his shoes. His feet still, and then he takes a step inside and closes the door.

"It explains some things, like why EEFS had a strict privacy agreement. But it raises even more questions."

"Connor still has the USB stick with the info he downloaded. It might have some answers. We could go look at it together," he offers.

"Connor's seen the files?" I freeze in shame.

"He had to. They were encrypted. But he was there, remember? He wants to help." Ryder puts on his best soothing tone.

"Great, I'm a nerd's dream come true," I grumble.

"Connor is cool about it. Trust me," Ryder says. His tone is so reassuring I believe him.

"A lot of crazy things now make sense. Like why I was so attracted to Colin straight away for one thing." I peer at him as a heated blush takes over my cheeks.

Ryder nods. "You didn't have a choice in the matter, did you?" A hopeful wisp abounds in his voice.

"Not really. But who we are is more than just DNA. At times in the back of my mind I thought it was all insane. For what it's worth, I'm sorry for what I put you through." I place my hand on his and the familiar warm glow travels up my body.

"It is all right." Ryder runs his hand through his hair. "Actually helps my ego a bit knowing it was truly not about me. For once it really was 'it is not you, it is me.'" It's a good joke, but I can't laugh. "So are you going to keep seeing Colin?"

"No way. I didn't fall in love with him— Imogene did. I inherited that from her. It's not my own."

As hard as it was to accept at first, I know I can't be with Colin, even if he wanted me. Saying it out loud helps. "Besides, I mightn't have been born in the conventional sense, but I was still born, and Imogene's my mother in a very real sense. A relationship with Colin would feel like a betrayal of her."

I wondered if my love for him isn't real, if it was manufactured as part of the cloning process. The pangs of love still stab at my heart when I think of him. I've no doubt in my mind that what Colin and Imogene had together was true love. Otherwise, I wouldn't have felt torn between him and Ryder. *Does that mean what I feel for Ryder could be true love?* I can't think about it now. It's too much.

"Are you going to tell him?" The question is innocent enough.

"No, it's all too much of a mess. I want to see him, to pick his mind about Imogene, and devour every morsel of information about her. But I don't think that's fair on Colin. It's like he's lost Imogene not once, but twice."

"What are you going to do if he tries to start something up with you again?"

"We can't be together, and that's how it has to be." I rub my arm, soothing away the goosebumps. "Can we talk about something else now?"

"Like, can we start over?" Ryder says in a tentative voice.

"You don't care what I am?" I whisper. "You don't care I'm a freakish abomination?"

Ryder rushes over to me. His arms wrap around me.

"*You* are *not* freakish, nor an abomination," he objects. "And I totally understand you falling into a shame spiral, but there was no need. You are awesome."

"But—" I protest.

"You are no more of a freak than me," he interjects, letting me go and taking a step away.

"What do you mean?"

"I was worried you would run from me if you knew."

He's here, knowing what I am. How could I desert him, no matter how bad? "There's no way I could run from you."

Ryder appears unsure, and then smirks. "Well, I might follow your lead and play show and tell."

A wave of crimson washes over me as his gaze lingers on my scar, peeking from the neck of my T-shirt. I'm surprised that wasn't enough to scare him off.

He stands up and goes to the center of my room. "Please, no spazzing out. I have no idea what is going on, but I have to share this with someone."

I hold my breath. Ryder begins to glow blue all over, and tiny electric sparks like mini lightning bolts bounce between his fingers. His eyes appear purple, and he seems to hover above the ground.

The hairs rise on my arms. My jaw dangles. "Ryder, what does this mean?"

He sets his jaw, grinding his teeth. "I have no idea, but I am going to find out." He stops shining, and his feet return to the floor. "But you see, you are not alone. I am different too, somehow. Someday, when I get to meet my mum, I will get some answers."

"So what do you know about your past so far?" I ask, trying to decide what it could mean.

"It has been hard to find out where I was originally from. There were some complications and a longer paper trail than with most adoptions." He doesn't hide the bitterness in his voice.

I mull over what he said, and then the penny drops. "You were returned?"

Ryder grimaces. "Multiple times." His eyes go to the floor. "Apparently, all the adoption mothers said I was too much of a demanding child to cope with. But eventually I found a home."

A crazy thought enters my head. I scan Ryder from head to toe. "Do you think you are like me?"

My voice cracks slightly. I can't bring myself to say the word *clone*.

"No," he says finally. "I was through a different agency, and I know the woman I remember was my real mum."

Even before breaking into EEFS, I had been so wrapped up in myself that I never gave much thought of what Ryder was going through. He barely spoke about his parents, adoptive or birth, other than his determination to locate his mother.

He brushes his hand through his hair and shifts uncomfortably. I've never seen him so vulnerable. I don't fight the urge to hug him. He reciprocates, and I squeeze him tighter.

"Ouch. Mishca, can you hug a little softer?" Ryder groans, but it morphs into a chuckle.

"Oops, sorry. I don't know my own strength." I let my arms fall away, but he grabs my hand.

"Got that right." He glances away. I sense guilt.

"Have you looked at the files?" There's no blame or anger.

"Just a little bit." He draws circles on my hand with his thumb.

"And?" I sit on the bed again. Isn't most bad news best taken sitting down?

"You *were* cloned, genetically modified, and planted as a sleeper." Ryder sits next to me.

"A sleeper?" The term sounds familiar, but I can't place it.

"A sleeper soldier, designed to be faster and stronger than a regular human, and then placed with a family. But your powers are not meant to manifest until you are activated for duty."

Hello, Syfy Channel.

"And yet I could kick your arse if I wanted to." I struggle to keep my voice even. Sometimes sarcasm is the best way to deal.

Ryder sits beside me. We both go quiet.

"So I'm faulty," I whisper, breaking the silence.

"What do you mean?"

"I haven't been activated. I'm defective." As I say the words, something twigs inside me. My mouth goes dry and bile rises up my throat.

"Mishca, what is it?" Ryder grabs my arm.

"I've heard that before. 'She's a defective human.' They were talking about me at the hospital and—" I lunge over to my cupboard where I had thrown in the package from Markus. I tear at the paper bag and snatch the business card. It has his name on it, a phone number, and a bible verse, Romans 8:1.

"He was there too," I exclaim, waving the business card around in Ryder's face.

"Slow down. Who was where?"

"The priest, Markus. He was at the hospital when you took me for my checkup, and again at the church today. He knew my name," I babble. "I didn't tell him, but he knew my name."

"Sounds like a real creeper." Ryder takes the business card from me and calls the number. He taps his foot and hangs up. "It went to voicemail."

I hunch down and let my head fall into my hands. "I don't know what to do." The words barely make it past my lips.

"The answers are in those files," Ryder says. "I am sure of it. How about tomorrow we go see Connor and —"

"Mishca," Mum calls from downstairs. "Dinner's ready."

"You'd better go," I say. Not that I want him to leave. I just don't want to go to a psychologist either, and keeping my parents happy will keep Dr. Usher at bay.

Ryder sighs. "Okay, but tomorrow? Connor has nearly cracked open all the files. You can get answers."

"I don't want to wait that long. Can we go tonight, after dinner? We can say we're going to the movies or something."

"Sure."

"Thank you." I carefully hug him. "One last thing. We're just friends." Although, my heart wants more, and it hurts to say it aloud, my head says I need time. "For now. I'm not ready to rush back into anything."

He nods. "I understand."

We walk down the stairs in silence. My parents watch us from the second we hit the bottom steps.

Ryder lingers at the front door. "Everything will be okay," he says solemnly, and then dashes down the stairs while I stand like a statue.

My heart flutters. A smile tugs at my lips. I walk into the dining room where Mum and Dad are already waiting. My pills sit next to my place.

"He didn't try anything funny, did he?" Dad curls his hands into fists.

"Tom!" Mum slaps him with a napkin.

"No, Dad. Everything's fine." *I wish.* I stab a piece of broccoli with my fork, and it cracks the plate. A tiny crack but still.

CHAPTER 31

I TOLD MY PARENTS that Ryder and I were going out for dessert and a movie. While the two of us are actually together, it's anything but romantic. This is *not* my idea of a date, sitting around a computer with someone I clearly make uncomfortable. Ryder lingers in the background as Connor takes me through the files. Perspiration drips down Connor's brow. He sneaks glances at me as though he could wish me away. I can't tell if he's scared or wants to study me. The idea of *anyone* putting me under the microscope makes me shudder.

Ryder's dining room has never felt so claustrophobic. Normally, I find the white walls and wooden cabinets charming. Tonight, they close in on me and remind me too much of hospitals. Even Jelly Roll, Ryder's dog, can't lift my spirits. He lies on the floor with his little legs sticking out from his stout body, sulking because I ignored his attempts to get belly rubs. I stand beside Connor, who hunches over the laptop set up on the dining room table. I'd prefer to be outside doing a perimeter sweep. Ryder leans against the kitchen bench. He believes I need space to process. At least, I hope that's what he thinks.

"I've cracked all the files I downloaded and searched them with a cross reference to your name and your code." Connor gulps and sneaks a glimpse at me.

I'm not going to bite your head off. "My code?" I ask, ignoring his cringing.

"Yes, your code. You're often referred to as AMR — Alpha Mishca Richardson. Alpha, because you're from the first batch of clones they made." Connor tries staring back at the computer but keeps looking at me out of the corner of his eye.

"How many other Alphas are there?" I ask, voice trembling. All the times I've been mistaken for someone else flash through my mind.

"There *were* lots, though your batch seems to be smaller than the ones that came after. You were the test run." Connor keeps his eyes forward.

"What do you mean 'were'?" Ryder chimes in.

"Most of them have died." Connor pauses before adding, "From a heart condition like Mishca's."

"How many?" I try to fight off the image of a pile of bodies that each has my face.

"Fifty," Connor says. He sounds too calm to me.

"How many sisters do I have left?" Both Ryder's and Connor's heads snap toward me. I don't understand why I have a sense of kinship to them, but I do.

"Four," Connor whispers. "There was five, but one died a month or so ago."

It's like I've been punched in the gut. Forty-five versions of me—dead. "What about my...I mean our mother?"

"She's why you all had the hole in your hearts. She had it originally. She died about a year after you were created. They stopped using her after the first batch. Not that they do more than two batches per original." He shrugs. "Can't have too many people out there all looking the same."

Ryder tries his best to comfort me as Connor's words sink in. While the original wasn't my mother in the traditional sense, she was the closest thing I was ever going to have to a birth mother, and I will never know her. I press my cheek into his chest. Inside, I'm numb.

After a moment, I push off Ryder. This is no time to be a sissy. Intel is the most important thing right now. Okay, since when has the word *intel* been in my vocab? "What else have you ascertained about me?"

Connor finally looks me square in the eye. Perhaps my show of emotions convinced him I wouldn't shoot the messenger or break his neck with my bare hands. "You've got a chip in your brain with a program that is set to trigger when you're activated."

"There's a chip?" My pitch elevates. "In my brain?"

Jelly Roll's ears prick up, and he peeks at me.

"Well, yes." Connor bites his lip.

Ryder rubs my arm. "It will be okay." He sounds so convincing I almost believe him.

I mull it over and decide I need answers. "What else?"

Connor clears his throat. "The program has two primary purposes: enhancement and control. Have you noticed any increases in speed, strength, hearing, and eyesight? Good at fighting? Suddenly know army stuff?"

I nod.

"Well, that's the program stimulating the genetic modifications that were made through the cloning process."

"And the control?" Ryder asks.

"Brainwashing," Connor replies. "From what I can gather, it seems to be based on a technique used on Korean prisoners of war. It aims to make the recipient feel overcome by guilt and a lack of self-worth so they're more pliable to suggestion and manipulation. Then, the clone undergoes reprogramming."

I shiver.

"Wait," says Ryder. "Nothing like that has happened."

"Yes, it has," I cut in. "My dreams."

"What dreams?" Connor asks.

Ryder clicks his fingers as though part of a puzzle has slid into place and nods.

"I didn't understand what they meant. I thought they were a side effect of the meds."

We lapse into an awkward silence. The three of us haven't moved or spoken for several minutes when Fin saunters into the room, his arm draped around a blonde.

"So you see babe—" He stops dead when he sees me, and then turns on his heel and flees the house, leaving the bewildered blonde behind.

"What's his problem?" she huffs before following after him.

I stare at Ryder.

"He refuses to talk about it," he says. "The files show Fin's father was the original Alpha male, like your, um, mum, and there are clones of his dad running around doing who knows what. But he—" Ryder cuts off and stares into the distance. I take a few steps over to him and squeeze his hand.

"We think Fin's dad was picked because of the genetic experiments the army did on him," pipes in Connor. "From my calculations, Fin was conceived before the cloning, but after the experiments." His voice softens. "And then, they killed his dad. His dad found out about the clones not long after the first batch was made, and they sent an assassin after him. I don't know how they managed to kill a genetically modified super solider, but they did."

"Fin's mum was pregnant with him at the time," Ryder adds. "He never knew his dad because of what these guys did to him."

"Does Fin know that?" I ask.

"Uh-huh."

It must be hard for Ryder to face that isolation. I'm the only one who knows his secret. Sometimes even best friends don't share everything. A pang of guilt hits me. I still haven't been able to bring myself to face Nerissa yet.

All of us go quiet after that. Outside, the blonde yells at Finlay, and there's the slamming of a car door.

I ignore the noise and focus on facts. Something about the Korean prisoner of war story hits home. "My dreams match the control methods," I say. "They're always about me not being good enough. But the program must have a glitch in it as no one's tried to reprogram me."

"That seems a bit excessive," Ryder says. "Why go to all the effort to reprogram you when they could have trained you from the start?"

"Money," Connor cuts in. "It costs money to raise an army from babies. By farming them out to families through EEFS, they don't have to pay to feed or clothe their soldiers. Not to mention how huge a facility it would have to be to house the people they create. That'd be pretty hard to keep secret."

My breath catches in my throat. I was created to be a soldier, in an army, to fight, to kill. "Who created me, Connor? What army am I meant to be a part of?"

"There wasn't much on that." Connor stares at the laptop. "The files I got were mainly about the programming and records on the alpha clones. But I did get a name — Wirth. He's the one who created you, and the cloning is his project. But it doesn't say why."

I chew on my thumbnail. *That name. Where have I heard it before?* After racking my brain for a few minutes, I give up. Everything hurts, especially my head and heart.

"And it also appears Wirth has raised one of your, ah, sisters himself — Othilia. She's his second-in-command now."

Connor holds out a photo. It's the "me" in black that I saw when I thought I was hallucinating. *She's been following me!*

"I need a break. It's too much." Ryder moves to follow. I put up my hand to stop him. "Give me a few minutes."

Jelly Roll ignores my desire to be alone and follows me, stopping at the door and flopping down. I step into Ryder's open-air gym, the anger swelling inside me and coiling in my muscles. I pull my arm back and let a right hook go at the punching bag. It flies off the hook, lands on the ground, and splits open. I stare, completely stunned, but probably shouldn't be surprised, all things considered. Thank goodness Ryder can get a discount on a new one.

"I thought I was the only one who could punch that hard before I met you." I spin at the voice. Finlay comes around the corner of the house out of the darkness. "I can run fast too. Teachers bugged me to apply myself. They reckoned I could have made the Olympics, and said I had natural talent. But I always wagged sports day. Now I wonder if anything was natural about it at all, or whether I inherited some of the freak juice they put in my father."

My mouth opens but closes immediately. I can't even hold his defiant stare.

"Then there's the army hand signals. I started doing them as a toddler. No one ever showed me 'cause my dad was already dead."

"I understand —"

"Your people destroyed my family," Fin hisses, "and I'll never forgive them for that."

"This happened to me too, Fin," I whisper. "I didn't do anything to your family."

His face stays like stone. "But you're one of them. You're unnatural. You're not even a human being."

Before I can respond, a fist connects with Finlay's jaw.

"I never want to hear you say that again," roars Ryder.

Fin spits out blood and wipes the remaining red from his chin. "She's an aberration, Ryder. Can't you see that? I don't want this thing in *my* house."

"Last time I checked, I owned this house," snarls Ryder. "Mishca can come here whenever she wants."

"You're going to choose *it* over me?" Finlay stares at Ryder bug-eyed.

"If you make me. She is a victim in this as much as you."

"Then I'm splitting." Finlay shoots me a glare that pierces through my heart before stomping off into the night.

Ryder comes straight to me with Fin's blood still on his fist. "Are you okay?"

I bite my lip. They shouldn't part ways over me. Although I protested my innocence, right now I *am* the monster.

Grabbing my hand, Ryder guides me into the kitchen. Connor scurries back to his seat. If he's trying to cover his eavesdropping, he needn't bother. I'd be surprised if the whole neighborhood hadn't heard the exchange.

"Here, drink this." Ryder hands me a glass of water.

I scull it robotically. Placing the glass on the sink, I take three deep breaths.

"Let's get back to it." My thoughts wander to my siblings.

"What does it say about the clo—Mishca's sisters?" Ryder has read my mind.

"They—the EEFSers for want of a better term—know about your heart transplant." Connor swivels around. "And that's keeping you safe. Same deal with Phanessa Jackson, who is now going by Othilia. Wirth fixed her heart personally and has been training her. But the other three, Michelle Cooper, Andrea Roberts, and Tammy Kanter, aren't so lucky. I don't know how to tell you this after everything else."

"What is it?" A knot tightens in my gut. "Tell me."

Connor's gaze meets mine, filled with a mixture of fear and sadness. "They're scheduled for termination next year."

"No." I look from Connor to Ryder. "I have to save them."

EPILOGUE

OTHILIA

How did I end up here again? I shoot dagger glares at the poor-little-rich-girl's house. *Bitch. Why is Wirth so interested in her when he has me?*

I lean against the smooth trunk of a large gum tree up in the branches, soaking in the quietness of the night and willing my emotions in check. Instincts need to guide me; my training needs to guide me. Not my feels for a weak defective human.

Most people would've made a lot of noise getting to this vantage point. But not me. I mastered moving silently a long time ago. From here, I can see the whole street. Being sent out on patrol is a relief. Wirth had been furious after the lab debacle.

Rage rumbles through my veins at the thought of the useless girl, and at Wirth for wanting her so badly, but mostly at myself for every time I slip and feel something other than hate for my supposed kin. *How can I care about someone who is so inferior?*

My ears prick at the sound of a car. It crawls down the street, its lights winking out before it stops close to the house I've been observing. My skin prickles. *Something is wrong.*

I whip out my phone and call headquarters. "Baker, get me a name for this plate," I bark before rattling off the numbers and letters. I draw a blank at the response. "Colin Read? It means nothing to me either."

I tap the phone against my chin. The person in the car is watching Mishca's house too. I slide down the tree to investigate.

This douche bag better not think I'm a hooker. I do my best to put on a smile before heading toward the car. After a few steps, the car door opens. A man steps out and turns to me with a confused, yet hopeful, expression like a stupid puppy that's been kicked and comes back for more. *He thinks he knows me.*

I stop midstride. *Boom-ba-boom.* My mouth fries and beads of sweat threaten to form. *Boom-ba-ba-boom.* I inhale a deep breath to calm my racing heart, but it won't still. My chest tightens and my stomach flips. *What is wrong with me?* I've never experienced anything like this before, and I don't like it one bit.

"Mishca? Oh, Mishca, I am so sorry. I know I freaked out on you twice, but please."

Her. Of course he thinks I'm her. I hate you. My mouth sets hard in a grimace. I hold up a hand. The man goes silent. *I love you.* The thought makes me want to punch myself in the face. He's in love with *her.* Every inch of my body knows it. Images of me tearing him apart with my bare hands bring back a smile. I move toward him like a lover would, gliding my hands around his neck as our bodies touch.

As we embrace, I angle my mouth to the man's ear, and whisper, "I'm not Mishca." My fingertips find the sweet spot, pinching a nerve in his neck. The man falls in a heap at my feet. *Where you should be.* I grin. Maybe things are starting to look up after all.

THE END

Thank you for reading! Find book two in the Open Heart series, SHATTERED, featuring tons of new challenges and heart-stopping action for Mishca and Ryder in 2016 catch the included special excerpt next!

Please sign up for the City Owl Press newsletter for chances to win special subscriber-only contests and giveaways as well as receiving information on upcoming releases and special excerpts.

www.sharonmjohnston.com

@ S_M_Johnston

All reviews are welcome and appreciated. Please consider leaving one on your favorite social media and book buying sites.

For books in the world of romance and speculative fiction that embody Innovation, Creativity, and Affordability, check out City Owl Press at www.cityowlpress.com.

Turn the page for a sneak peek at the next book in
the Open Heart series,

SHATTERED

BY: SHARON M. JOHNSTON

Coming Soon from City Owl Press

CHAPTER 1

MY SISTERS ARE going to be murdered. And I don't know if I'm enough to save them. But I have to try.

The scenarios of how I can rescue them play in my mind during the long drive to Nerissa's place, even though I try to block them out. I occupy the time with anything other than the image of my clone sister on death row. A shining and levitating Ryder — total surprise the first time I saw that supernatural trick — edges into my thoughts. I smile at the odd but welcome vision. Then, my heart wrenches over the barrier between us. A barrier he doesn't even know exists. At Sophitia's request I've kept their joined heritage a secret. It feels like a betrayal. It *is* a betrayal. And truth be told, I've betrayed him enough.

Colin flashes into the mix. I wince at the intrusion. I want to travel back in time and bitch-slap past me for ever believing that Imogene's love for Colin was my own. I can't believe I pushed Ryder away for so long for a stupid crush that didn't belong to me. It was my…mother's, well the person who they copied me from anyway. The emotions belonged to her, not me.

Ugh. The spinning jumble of stuff in my head is making me nuts. But the thought of telling Ryder the truth scares me more than anything. My insides squirm every time I envision how the conversation with him would go. If I do tell him, he mightn't come with me to rescue my sisters. And I don't know if I've got the courage to do it without him. My soldier instincts keep kicking in more often, but each time my humanity slips. For the past two weeks, Ryder has been my anchor to normality. Without him, I'm vulnerable.

I've kept everyone else at a distance, hoping the space will help me work my shit out. But I now know I need people in my life more than ever. I can't do this all on my own.

My hand finds the gear stick to put it into fourth. The action ignites a memory, and finally brings back a grin. On one of Ryder and my first dates, Finlay, his best friend, had tagged along. Fin insisted he always rode shotgun, forcing me to move over the middle of the bench seat with my legs on either side of the gear stick. I never expected to have Ryder's hands between my legs that early in our relationship or with an audience. I miss him, his touch. *Just get back together with him already. You know he still wants you.*

I let free a laugh. A normal, girl—that's what I felt like then, when I was with Ryder. I might never feel that way again. My mood deteriorates to sombre. Maybe I'd be better ending it for good. *Will I even be able to help my sisters with or without him?* I'm an abomination after all.

A truck comes towards me in the other lane. I imagine steering the car in front of it. How easy it would be.

Suck it up, soldier. This pity party is over.

I shake my head as though that will make the intrusive thoughts dissipate. The best thing might be to think of nothing at all, so I distract my wayward mind with loud music and try to focus on the road. The farther I drive, the houses decrease and the trees increase. I slow down. A mailbox shaped like a shell sits in front of a long driveway. The road is hedged by masses of giant gums.

I turn in and continue down the path, surrounded by shadows and trees. The sunlight throws glare through the windscreen as the car comes into the clearing. A large two-story home, made of wood with large verandas and covered in fairy lights, is nestled in the middle.

I kill the ignition on Mum's car. Betsy is too conspicuous for me to be driving around now. The soldier side of me has a red alert melt down whenever I contemplate driving my hot pink car. My fists clench and unclench, leaving fingernail crescent marks in my palms.

No putting this off any longer. Go in there and get your best friend back. Grovel if necessary.

Despite the urge to avoid any potential conflict and flee, I get out of the car and head for the front door. My hand lifts to knock as the door swings open. Nerissa's brother, Dorian, has the back of his head to me as he yells up the hallway. "Mum, do you need me to bring anything from the shops?"

A faint "no" floats down the hall to us. My feet and mouth refuse to move, and Dorian crashes into me as he runs out.

"Omph." We fall in a pile; unfortunately, he lands on top. His large frame crushes me. His blue eyes sparkle a cloudy grey today.

"Mishca?" He jumps off me, and then offers a hand. "Are you okay?"

I brush myself off. "Yeah, I'm fine."

"That's not what I mean." His stare pierces me. The overprotectiveness vibe I got from him that night when we all went out has gone, and I'm left wondering why. "You've been through some heavy stuff this year. Are you *okay*?"

My stomach swirls with anxiety like there's a mini black hole in there wanting to suck me inside. *How could she tell him?* I know Dorian and Nerissa are close, but this isn't her secret to tell.

Inside the hard-arse me and the scared-to-shit me battle for control. The soldier wins. "As best as could be expected." I can't say the reality aloud.

Dorian gives me a half smile. "Well, it totally wasn't cool for that Colin dude to treat you like that." I flinch at the name of my original's soul mate, and my almost lover. Then a weight on my shoulders lightens. He doesn't know what I am. He glances up the hallway.

"Nerissa will be so happy to see you. She's missed you so much." I've somehow managed to pass the are-you-good-enough-to-be-friends-with-my-sister test, and all I had to do was get screwed over by a guy. He sticks his head back inside and yells, "Hey, nerd-burger! Mishca's here."

The thumping of feet follow his words. *How can someone so light make so much noise?* A squeal escapes Nerissa's mouth as she sees me. She's on me in a couple of strides. I reciprocate her hug but release her when she winces.

"Let's go out the back." She grabs my hand and drags me through the house. When we've settled under the pergola beside their large lagoon, Nerissa stares at me with pain evident in her eyes. "I've missed you."

She could've said much worse.

"I know." I look away. I can't keep my gaze on her without my heart wanting to shatter into a million pieces.

"How's everything going?"

I flex my fingers. "Better. I know I'm the worst," I pause and have to force the words past my lips, "I'm the worst person in the world for ignoring your calls and messages straight after. And for not coming to see you sooner. I just couldn't face you...or anyone. I needed some time."

"It's okay." The sincerity on her face compounds my guilt.

"Mum and Dad were the hardest. I'm still so scared they're going to discover the truth. How could they want me if they know?"

She squeezes my hand. "Give them a little more credit than that. Do you think they'd be scared off by how you were born?" *Created*, I correct her silently. She continues, "Everybody's got something about them. Some secret they never want to see the light of day."

"Oh yeah?" I challenge. "What's yours?"

"You know mine," Nerissa replies, staring anywhere but at me, and then focuses on something to her left.

"Oh yeah, how goes the wedding plans?"

"Faster than I'd like."

"Do you love Dylan, or are you just with him for your parents?"

She doesn't reply straight away. *Mishca, you are such a schmuck for bringing that up.*

"Yeah, I love the big lout. I guess we're lucky

that it's not a situation where we're strangers when it's our time to tie the knot."

"So that's it?" I ask, scrunching up my nose. "You've got an arranged marriage? I thought there might have been something else as well, something more," I incline my head, thinking how to phrase it right, and then say simply, "serious."

Her eyes won't meet mine again. This time she looks to her right, shaking her head. "Yeah, that's my big secret." She scratches her nose and tries to smile but only her lips move, nothing else lights up. I know for certain Nerissa is lying to me, but I don't call her on it now. She embraces me. "I don't care about any of that stuff with you. You have to believe me."

"I know that now. I'm sorry I didn't give you more credit." I give her an extra squeeze, careful not to be too hard.

Her words and body language run through my head. She's not lying about being betrothed to Dylan. When she looked to her left, it meant she was recalling something real and telling me the truth. But when she replied that her arranged marriage was her big secret she glanced to her right, scratched her noise, and reinforced my question. *Hold up – I'm a human lie detector too?* My freakiness never ceases to amaze.

"I'm glad you've been in contact with Ryder. He was so worried. You know he called me a zillion times."

I almost flinch. It hadn't occurred to me the two of them would be in contact. *Of course they would talk to each other. Who wouldn't after what happened? And they both care about you.*

"We pulled a Nancy Drew on the files yesterday," I say, keen to change the topic.

Nerissa's eyes widen.

"And?"

I fill her in: the discover of my sister clones, the death of one of them, and the termination sentence for the others.

"That's horrible! They're going to kill those girls?"

"Not if we can get to them first. Are you up for a road trip?"

She claps her hands. "Where to?"

"Mackay, Airlie Beach, and Townsville," I reply.

"I could definitely think of worse places to go." She pulls out her laptop. "When."

"As soon as possible. We can't be certain, but Connor found an itinerary that hits all three spots at the beginning of next week. Even though it says they're not scheduled for termination until next year."

"Dylan would probably have to come, are you cool with that?" she asks. I go rigid at the thought of another person knowing my secret. She must have noticed because she blurts out, "I haven't told him your secret, and I won't. All being well we won't have to either."

The tension disintegrates from my body. "That's good. I've already asked Ryder. That'll balance things and not raise suspicion from my parents."

"Good. Let's do some research. We need to look at flights and somewhere to stay. I agree the sooner the better. Next week would be great. I won't be too far into the uni term for it to matter."

Nerissa gets in her zone, making lists and preparing our itinerary. I lie on her bed and prop my head up on my hand, making suggestions where I can. She definitely wants to help, and everything else she has said is genuine. A heavy weight rests on my heart that she doesn't trust me enough to tell me what's really going on, especially with what she knows about me. I want to confront her, but I won't jeopardise the plan to save my sisters. After about half an hour, the boredom of planning overtakes me, and my eyelids get heavy. My blinks get longer until my lids don't reopen, and I succumb to sleep.

Ryder, Ryder where are you? Fog against black. Nerissa? Anybody? Mist and darkness surround me. I stumble forward. Please don't leave me, I'm sorry. My hands reach out into the black, groping for anything. But there is nothing.

"Forget Ryder. He'll leave you, abandon you. Just like Colin and your mother." The voice snakes through my mind. My temples throb.

I'm confused. Mum has never left me. I clutch handfuls of hair as I curl into a ball, praying the voice will go away. The dreams feel worse when he's in them.

"Not her. Not the one pretending to be your mother. Your real mother." I recoil at his invasion of my thoughts. "You prayers won't save you. Give in now. Come to me."

"No!" I run away from the voice, stumbling as I go. Then, the man with the long brown hair materializes before me.

"Run if you like, Mishca. I will always be able to catch you." He sniggers. "Always."

I wake with a start. Drool trickles from the corner of my mouth. I wipe it off with the back of my hand. The dreams no longer get to me now that I know they're just some bogus programming. I won't let them beat me. I try to remember the details of the man's face—he has to be Wirth—but it's all a blur.

"Are you okay?" asks Nerissa.

"Yeah, I'm fine." I try to smooth down my messy curls. "Are you sure your parents will be okay with this?"

Nerissa nods. "I'm going to pitch it as a birthday treat. They know Dylan will protect me." She grins wickedly, so unlike the angelic look that's her default setting. "I know Dylan will do just about anything I ask."

"Even a north Queensland road trip?"

"Yep. But we'll only have to do a little bit of

driving. We can fly direct to Mackay at the end of the week, and then drive to Townsville with a stop off at Airlie on the way. We catch another direct flight home. We've just got to hire a car for the drive and find a place to stay. Caravan parks seem to be the cheapest if we book a cabin or villa."

I sit still, surprised at myself. "So we're really going to do this?"

"As long as you can convince your parents." Nerissa knows how overprotective they can be, just like hers. "How are you going to tackle them?"

"I'll ask tomorrow. I'm hoping they'll be in a receptive mood."

"Sounds like a plan."

She reaches over to her drawer and pulls out a present the size of a shoebox wrapped in blue paper with penguins on it. "Here. It was meant to be for your birthday, but I was hoping it would show you that we're still good—no matter what."

"You didn't have to," I say, flushed with embarrassment. "I haven't even gotten you anything yet and your birthday is...," I count in my head, "Thursday!"

My sad sackness has thrown my usual effective present shopping out the window. I tear at the paper to reveal a pair of gorgeous blue sapphire huggies. I slip them in, clipping each one in place.

"That's okay. What kind of best friend would I be if I got angry at you for forgetting with everything that's going on?"

"You still think of me as your best friend?" I ask with a sheepish drop of my chin.

She gives me a smile, her whole face lighting up, and looks me in the eye. "Of course."

I hug her, forgetting to be gentle.

"Ouch, Mishca!"

"Whoops. Sorry."

Nerissa bites her lip and glances at me. "Do you really think you can save them?"

I shrug. "I don't know. But I have to try."

ACKNOWLEDGEMENTS

It takes a ciliate to create a book, but in my case it was a bustling metropolis that contributed to making DIVIDED a reality.

She-Who-Must-Not-Be-Named (she's very shy), thank you for being my original Alpha reader, and nagging me for more chapters. I hope you love Sophia because she is for you.

Wendy Higgins, you were the first person to beta read for me, but beyond that you have been a great source of strength and comfort.

Evie, thank you for all your support, both as a reader, designer, and as a friend.

Angela Slatter, thank you for mentoring me and pushing me with my words.

Aimee, Nicola, Lauren, Ros & Mum (and anyone else who read DIVIDED that I've missed), thanks for being the extra set of eyes on my story.

To everyone on Inkpop who supported my writing, back when this story was known as MISHCA. I love you guys and miss the community.

Sommies, you know you rock my world. Thank you for all the love and support over the years.

My YAtopians, both past and present, your support and friendship has meant so much. My Aussie Owned & Read gals, so glad you found me and took me into your fold. Love you guys.

Stacey Nash, Jeyn Roberts, Lauren McKellar - I heart you guys big time.

Big love to my fellow Pitch Wars mentors and Pitch Madness hosts. I love the community we share. A big thank you to Brenda Drake for all the support you've given me and the faith you've had in me.

To the Disenchantments crew - we will rock on.

Tina Moss, you found me in amongst the Twitter pitches and I'm so glad you did. You've handled my baby with care. I couldn't ask for a better editor. And your cover design skills rock.

Mum, you are an amazing woman and an amazing mother. Dad, I miss you. God, thank you for giving me my crazy brain with weird stories inside.

Hubby, you are my one and only forever. Thank you for putting up with my writing obsessiveness that has cut into family time. Thank you for being my ideas sounding board. Thank you for loving me and being my anchor. Love you forever, Babe.

ABOUT THE AUTHOR

From sunny Queensland, Australia, Sharon M. Johnston writes weird stories and soulful contemporaries. Working as a PR specialist by day, in her spare time she writes, blogs, plays with her fur babies, and enjoys computer games with her family. A regular host of Pitch Madness and a Pitch Wars mentor, a runner-up in The Australian Literary Review's short story competition, and a blogger with YAtopia and Aussie Owned & Read, she's a versatile artist. Well known for her sense of style, she's been stalked by women wanting to know where she buys her shoes.

www.sharonmjohnston.com

CPSIA information can be obtained
at www.ICGtesting.com
Printed in the USA
FSOW01n2226270116
16289FS

9 780986 251634